JOHN ADAMS

Young Revolutionary

Illustrated by Meryl Henderson

JOHN ADAMS

Young Revolutionary

by Jan Adkins

ALADDIN PAPERBACKS

New York London Toronto Sydney Singapore

First Aladdin Paperbacks edition June 2002
Text copyright © 2002 by Jan Adkins
Illustrations copyright © 2002 by Meryl Henderson

ALADDIN PAPERBACKS
An imprint of Simon & Schuster Children's Publishing Division
1230 Avenue of the Americas
New York, NY 10020

Designed by Lisa Vega
The text of this book was set in New Caledonia.

Printed in the United States of America
2 4 6 8 10 9 7 5 3 1

LCCN available from the Library of Congress

ISBN 0-689-85135-9

ILLUSTRATIONS

CONTENTS

The Marsh

John Adams was hiding. He was under a bundle of reeds next to a little marsh island and a flock of ducks. They weren't real ducks. They were painted wooden ducks John had carved out of cedar and pine. He hoped that real ducks would see them and think this marsh was a good place for a rest and some food. He struggled to be quiet and patient, but John was worse than almost anybody in Massachusetts at silence and patience.

Then the ducks came. John threw off the reeds just as the ducks skimmed in for a landing.

Tick, boom!

The sound of his flintlock shotgun rolled across

the marsh. He picked up the other shotgun and fired again.

Tick, boom!

The ducks flapped hard and turned sharply toward the ocean, gone. White, bitter powder smoke hung over the water in front of the reeds, drifting across the wooden ducks and the two dead mallards floating near them. John laughed and shouted, "Ducks for dinner!" He loved hunting in the marsh, shooting well, bringing down game for the table. The Adams family would eat roast duck the next night.

He threw the rest of the reeds off his boat. It was a little, squat boat shaped like a pumpkin seed. It had taken John and his friends Tom Bass and Tim Quincy far out into Massachusetts Bay to watch finback whales rolling and blowing their way north. It had taken them up the big outer harbor and around the city of Boston, up into the Charles River behind it. It was their adventure boat.

"There, now, put both shotguns down here where the spray won't rust them. Cover them over, just so," he told himself. He was careful about the shotguns. They were dangerous and precious. They were important to his whole family.

He paddled the pumpkinseed boat out of the reeds and picked up the decoys, one by one. "Good work, my boys," he told the wooden ducks. Attached to each decoy was a tarred string tied to a stone, so it wouldn't float away. He wrapped the string carefully around each duck so he could float his wooden flock again without tangles. He arranged them all in a big canvas bag and shoved them up under the forward deck of the boat. John liked things laid out neat.

"Well, my oh my," he said as he picked up the dead ducks. "My oh my, you are beautiful, aren't you? I'm sorry to bring you down, you beauties, but we do love duck. Why, if you ever tasted my mother's duck gravy, you wouldn't mind at all, I assure you." Their whites and blacks and greens were so clean and bright. He looked at the ducks in the way any good hunter looks at his game: a little sadly, a little proudly. He felt strangely connected to the ducks. He wanted to thank them.

John had Ponkapoag Indian friends. In the

summer when their tribe fished and dug clams at the seashore, he'd seen old men return the clamshells and fish bones to the water after the tribe had eaten. Old Amos Ahanton had scattered them while speaking in the Ponkapoag language. John asked his friend Hezakiah what he was saying.

"He's thanking them for the food. Telling them how delicious they were. Asking them to come back again and feed us."

John felt that way about the ducks too.

He raised the boat's stumpy mast and set its sail. John sat in the stern and held the tiller to steer. He swung the boat around a shoal of grasses and into the deeper water of the inlet and headed for home.

Behind him, beyond the dunes and tidal flats to the north, was the great city of Boston, where as many as ten thousand people lived. To John's left, eastward across the marsh, were Massachusetts Bay and the Atlantic Ocean. To his right, lumpy on the western horizon, were the Blue Hills. Beyond them lay the deep, untraveled wilderness of America. John had heard some folks say that a

squirrel could start in the maple and spruce woods of those hills and travel from tree to tree all the way to the fabled Mississippi River without ever touching ground.

"Far enough and shallow enough," John announced. Pushing the tiller over hard, he brought the boat up into the wind. It stopped as the canvas sail flapped noisily without the shoulder of the wind in it. John stood and wrapped the sail around the mast. He tied it snug and lifted the mast out of its socket, sliding it up under the forward deck, then drew out a push-pole. He pulled up the centerboard and poled the boat up Town Brook. Standing with his head just below the level of the grasses, he poled up through the Adams farm, all the way to a sandy turn near the town landing. He tied the boat up to its stake at the brook's edge and unloaded the next day's duck dinner and the shotguns. He laid the guns with the powder horn and the shot bag on his coat to keep them dry, and tied an old, patched square of canvas over the open cockpit. He squinted toward the North.

"No doubt," John said, "it's comin' on to blow. Maybe rain too. Sure as dogs and fleas. Ayuh."

John looked at the sky and smelled the cold front's wind. *Why not get a swim in now before it got too cold?* he thought. He took off every stitch and waded into the creek. He was small for eleven. Built like a stocky little terrier, tough as cut nails. John loved to swim. He could swim for miles; maybe all the way to Boston.

This was the place he loved most in the world, this marsh. He never wanted to leave it.

It was getting on to suppertime. John dried off in the wind and put his clothes back on. He cleaned and plucked the ducks. Then he walked up to the town landing carrying his family's shotguns and his ducks, singing as if he were the happiest boy in Massachusetts. Maybe he was.

There was some daylight left and time before supper. John took the long way home through the village.

"Good evening to ye, Widow Bass," John called out and dipped his head politely. "Thy beach roses and hollyhocks look glorious this day."

The old woman was feeding her chickens in the side yard of her tiny cottage. Her curtsy was stiff but it still had some of the grace learned from many country dances. "Yes, John Adams, they come along. Not near as fine as last year. Nossuh." The Widow Bass spoke with the same Yankee twang and long vowels as John. "But the Lord brings us what He will. You take my g'day to y'mothah, and bless you."

"My thanks, Widow Bass." He waved as he continued. John Adams was always polite. Even when he was throwing snowballs, wrestling, or insulting one of his friends, he was remarkably courteous. That's the way Braintree folks had to be.

They blessed one another partly as a polite form of greeting, but it was far more than that. Braintree was a Puritan village, a tight, intense community. Every person was part of its success or failure, and every person was responsible for his or her conduct. For these people, God was close, a part of everything they did—their chores, their farming, their meals, their singing in the fields. The Devil was just as close. Life was a constant struggle between God and the Devil, good and evil, and the battleground was the human heart.

A horse overtook him at the crossroads. It was John Quincy's chestnut hunter, broad in the chest, well muscled, a rich man's horse with a fine English saddle. John had seen his father stitching and repairing that saddle, and he knew the man in it. John stopped and bowed, "Good day to thee, Squire Quincy."

John Quincy reined up. "And to thee, young Adams. Plump brace of ducks you've brought out of the marsh. Was that your whole bag for the day?"

"Enough is as good as a feast, sir."

"True enough, yessuh. You remember me to y'fathah, heah? You're becoming a fine hunter, young man. You'll be a fine militiaman, like y'fathah. Bless ye now."

"And you, sir."

Quincy headed east for his big house. Quincy was one of the important men of Braintree, and of Massachusetts. He'd been speaker of the Massachusetts Assembly for many years.

John walked on.

"G'day, John!" It was Amos. They fished and dug for clams together.

"Amos! Look at these ducks. So fat they near swamped the boat when they splashed down. Look at that. I could feed four families with these two ducks."

"Go on! Nossuh! You hear about the Allens' horse?" Amos asked.

John shook his head.

"Gone. Busted up the fence and headed for the Blue Hills. Not so good. Panther or a bear could get it, easy."

"Maybe he'll get Hezakiah Squamogg to track it, run it down before it comes to evil." John knew that some of the Ponkapoags still had the old ways, and they knew the forest beyond the Blue Hills better than anyone.

"Good thought. You see him, you should tell 'im."

"See you at meeting, Amos."

Amos walked off toward his father's tannery at the south end of town. John continued toward the village center.

The center of Braintree, its active heart, was the

meeting house—their church and town hall, all in one. It was sturdy, covered with white clapboards, and except for its big windows it hadn't a hint of decoration. It was as plain and honest as the Puritans who built it a few years before John was born. This was where the business of the town got done. This was where John Adams learned about God and government.

"John Adams!"

He jerked around; it was the Widow North. "G'day to ye, Widow North."

"Dost thee think it proper to walk through the town with thy sleeves all undone and thy shirt not buttoned proper?" She was speaking to him in the old formal language, so he knew she was serious.

The people of Braintree were practical, realistic families who knew how easy it was to make mistakes. They also believed in forgiving mistakes. They were thoughtful, intelligent, and they talked a lot. To make the difficult climb away from the Devil they were willing, even eager, to talk about morality and immorality—not only in themselves but in others as well.

"I apologize if I have offended thee, Widow North."

"It shows a lack of modesty, young Adams, and a lack of pride in thy family to go about undone and tatty. Your good father would not have thee dress like a swineherd. Do up your shirt and jacket, now. Here, I'll hold thy ducks and guns."

John rearranged his shirt, did up the buttons, tied up his sleeves, and straightened his jacket. "I thank thee for correcting me, Widow."

"We all need correction of a day, John. Here, then. Fine ducks."

"Thank ye."

"God bless ye now, John Adams, and bless your family."

"And you, and yours, Widow." John bowed amiably, took his shotguns, and went on his way. He scowled. Not at the Widow North but at himself. He should have thought of his appearance, walking through town!

John walked past the village pump and horse trough, set under a tree in front of a tavern. The taverns were part of the town's business too, where

12

travelers with news from other towns paused to eat, or sip a tankard of ale made by John's uncles.

"Mister Bradley," John spoke to Hops Bradley, a white-haired man dozing against the tavern wall in the last light.

The old man started from sleep and looked around him. "What's that? What's about? Is that you, young Adams?"

"Yessuh. Did the day go well for ye, Mister Bradley?"

"Good enough. Pains and misery is the life of old men, Adams. Stay young."

"Yessuh. Might I help you in some way, sir?"

The old man was grumpy but kind, "Mebbe', just mebbe' you can. Help an old man up, Adams."

John shifted the shotguns carefully and braced Hops Bradley, pulling him up from the hard bench.

Hops groaned. "Fell asleep after the wind shifted into the north. Had a warm spot on the south wall, here."

"Yessuh, Mister Bradley. Could ye suggest what the weather will be?" John knew that old men could tell by experience and by the throb in their bones what was coming over the horizon. Braintree was a rural town of farmers, fishermen, and craftspeople; their lives were intimately dependent on the weather.

Bradley looked at the clouds, sniffed, and looked for birds. "Rain on Thursday, cold and dry tomorrow," he said after a time. "Good time for bottom fishing off Squantum on Thursday morning, though."

"I'd be pleased to sail you up to Squantum, Mister Bradley." Squantum was the long neck of land that reached out into the harbor above Braintree.

Hops squinted one eye. "You goin' to school up to Master Cleverly's now, yes?"

"Yessuh," John said, unhappily, but Hops didn't notice his tone, or chose not to notice it.

"Learn somethin', then. No time for flat fishin' if you're learnin' your primer." The old man squinted into the north, toward the oncoming clouds and the cold front. "But if ye do go bottom fishin', you could bring me back a nice witch flounder f'my suppah."

14

John smiled, "If I do go, I'll bring ye a fine flounder, sir. Lean on me, if ye will, and we'll get down the lane to your cottage."

When Hops Bradley had blessed him and gone into his cottage, John walked on a little faster. The sun was setting, workmen were losing their light. All over Braintree, farmers were coming back from their fields with their horses or oxen. Fishermen had sold their catch early in the afternoon but used the afternoon light to work on their boats and tackle; they were returning to their homes too. While the blacksmith was banking his fires for the night, the potter was stoking his kiln fire for an overnight burn. With the dimming of the light, folks were leaving work for the evening meal. John's home and his family were just ahead at the turn of the road. He was part of the evening homecoming, part of Braintree, Massachusetts.

The Saltbox

The Adams house was as plain as the meeting house. The main part of the two-floor house was built by John's great-grandfather. John's grandfather added a kitchen addition at the back and continued the rear roofline down low to cover it. Folks called this kind of high-front, low-back house a saltbox, because it looked like the hinged pine box that kept salt by the kitchen fire.

John walked around the house to his father's workshop. This late in the day the shop was dim. It smelled deeply of leather and oil and beeswax. New and repaired shoes hung in pairs from oak beams. Harnesses for horses and oxen hung in long, dark strips. The floor was swept, the cobbler's bench was clean, and the tools were racked in rows. *Deacon John Adams the shoemaker is out,* John thought as he headed to the house, *and Selectman John Adams is on town business.*

When John opened the heavy front door, the fragrance of bread and chowder met him like a hug.

"There you are, John! At last! And haven't I had the meal ready for an age and more? And where were you when I needed kindling wood?"

"I apologize, mother." John knew that Susanna Boylston Adams had plenty of kindling. He had filled the kitchen firkin on Monday. His younger brothers Peter and Elihu waved hello at him, silently, as his mother scolded on.

"And here I was, tending the family and keeping the home together without as much help as a goat would give. And your father off spending more time on Braintree's poor and feebleminded than on his own family. The comfort of the grave is all I can hope for, and no thanks before it."

"I thank thee, Mother. I thank thee for the meal

that smells so fat and fine. And I thank thee for the comfort you give us."

"Oh, yes, I make a home for you but I do it on next to nothing, on a few shillings. The rest goes to the church and the poor right out of your father's hands, like water out of a sieve. And aren't we just about the poorest clutch of ragamuffins in the town? I ask you."

But she really wasn't asking him. She was fretting and scolding as she often did. John knew they were not the poorest family in Braintree. They had a home and they didn't lack for food.

John heard the front door open and close just as his mother was lighting a pair of candles. She went on to close the heavy curtains against the cold night, hoarding all the warmth the house would hold.

"Who's that, then?" she called.

"And who would it be, woman? Old King George?" Deacon Adams came into the kitchen with his cheeks pink from the cool wind. He had a sad, kind face with a high forehead over bright, jolly eyes. He picked up Elihu immediately and tickled Peter under his arm. The boys were delighted to see their father. Still carrying Elihu he collared John and hugged him close. "And how was your day in the marsh, John?"

"Very fine, sir." Though John and his father were close and affectionate, they spoke formally to one another. It was the old way and it pleased them both. "And profitable, sir." He held up the brace of ducks his mother had ignored.

"Look at these, Susanna! Fat ducks for tomorrow's supper from our master hunter."

Susanna look back briefly and with disapproval, "Hardly worth the wood to cook 'em."

"I think not. They seem like a feast for just five Adamses. P'raps we might think of asking the Weld girls to join us, so soon after they've lost their parents. Show them a little warmth and fill their bellies."

"Mr. Adams, must you herd every unfortunate of Braintree through my kitchen?" Susanna addressed her husband as "Mr. Adams" when anyone was near, even their children. This, too, was an old way of speaking but it did not please Deacon Adams as much.

"Come, now, they have little in this world and we have so much."

"So much, indeed, Mr. Adams. I can tell ye that I was accustomed to more in this world before I came to the wilderness to make you a home, sir."

There was silence for a moment, and then Deacon Adams burst into laughter, followed by John and his brothers. The notion of Braintree as "the wilderness" was so far-fetched that it was funny. Not a day's walk from Boston, one of the wealthiest cities in the New World, they were far from the Indian battles of the real frontier, hundreds of miles inland.

Susanna Adams was not always such a scold. Sometimes she fell into a gloom and wouldn't say a word for days. Sometimes she could be as gay and silly as a girl. She was a puzzling woman.

"Look at this meal!" Deacon Adams said heartily, hoping to please his fussy young wife. "This is my favorite of all the good meals you set before us, Susanna. Fresh bread, sweet butter. Is that thy glorious plum jam? And there's your sublime chowder, the food of the angels."

Susanna nodded with her lips pursed. She would not argue with Deacon Adams further. He was a calm, even man with enormous patience. "That," John promised himself, "is something I must learn from him." But there was a point at the far end of that patience where the good man's anger would explode. John had seen it only a few times and it was frightening. It was not the meaningless rage of a casually violent man, it was the powerful right-eousness of a man who would bend his principles only so far and not a barleycorn more.

The Adams kitchen, like most of the homes in Braintree, was centered—the whole house was centered—on a massive brick and fieldstone fire-place. The shoulder-high mouth of the fireplace was fitted with a spit for roasting meat, swinging wrought-iron hangers that held iron pots over the heat, and end irons that kept logs from rolling across the stone hearth and onto the wide-board pine floor. At the back of the fireplace a rectangu-lar cast-iron fireback was set into the brick; it reflected the heat back into the room better than brick. Inside the fireplace to one side was the oven, like an arched brick cave with an iron door. In the morning, Susanna had built a very hot fire in the oven with dry twigs, adding to them as they burned down. When the bricks inside the oven were shimmering with heat, she scraped the coals into the fireplace. Then she slipped the loaves of bread dough into the oven on a long-handled elm spatula, a "peel." The iron door was swung shut, and the heat of the bricks baked the bread.

Susanna used a hooked stick to swing the big iron pot out into the kitchen and to lift the lid from the pot. She ladled chowder into deep pottery bowls. Chowder was a whole meal, thick with potatoes, leeks, fish, pounded biscuit, and herbs. The leeks and potatoes were from the Adams garden. The milk came from Sweet Anne, their jersey cow.

The bread was wheat and cornmeal sourdough, sweetened with molasses. As John and his brothers set the table with napkins and pewter spoons, Deacon Adams cut the bread into thick, crusty slices. Susanna poured cool cider into stoneware mugs.

The Adams sat and held hands as Deacon Adams blessed the food. "Give us Thy blessing with this meal. May our hands do Thy work and our hearts know Thy bidding. Grant us a bit more patience with one another, so that husband and wife quarrel not and understand one another more sweetly." John heard his mother squirm in her chair. "Bless Peter for his good watchfulness over his brother Elihu, and give him more awareness in meeting, so that he does not fidget like a hungry squirrel during prayer." Peter snorted, suppressing his laughter, though Deacon Adams was not against laughing in God's presence. "Bless our Elihu for learning so much of his ABC's, Lord. He is a bright, good boy, and we know he will no longer cast rocks and sticks at the chickens." Elihu let out a little moan. "Yes, Lord, we know that he is a good boy and will probably ask Thy forgiveness for unkindness against chickens in his bedtime prayers. Bless our fine son John and his keen shooting eye, and perhaps he will have an eye just as keen for attending Mr. Cleverly's school, where he should have been instead of hunting in the

marsh." Now it was John's turn to squirm in his chair. "Thank Thee for our prosperity in goods and love, for our friends in Braintree and Boston, and for our work. Bless those less fortunate, like the Weld girls, and strengthen our hearts to lend them our help."

"And deliver us," Susanna Adams broke in, "from eating cold chowder."

"Yes, Lord," Deacon Adams prayed with a smile in his voice, "we know that cold chowder is an abomination in Thy sight, so bless us all. And amen."

The family echoed the father's "amen" and set to the chowder.

After dinner Susanna heated water and made a pot of tea. She mixed hot water with well water and dipped some of her own soft soap from a pottery jar to wash the dishes.

Deacon Adams lit a small fire in the parlor fireplace—each room on the ground floor had its own fireplace and its own flue, contributing to the great, beehive-shaped brick center of the house. John mixed boiling water from the kitchen pot with soft soap and carried it into the parlor with a scrap of linen rag. Deacon Adams sat in his high-backed rocking chair and placed the now-short kitchen candle beside him, close enough that he could read. Peter brought the leather-bound Bible, and Elihu climbed up into his father's lap beside the big book. When Susanna sat beside the deacon with her knitting, he began to read.

This was one of John's favorite times of day, listening to his father's deep voice and the noble rhythm of the Bible language. He scrubbed the shotguns' barrels with soap and water so the spent powder acids wouldn't pit the smooth bores. He dried the bores with a clean rag and coated them with fish oil to protect them from rust.

By the time John was finished with the shotguns, Elihu was asleep. The deacon stood with the little boy and presented him, still asleep, to his mother for a kiss.

Peter kissed his mother goodnight, and she hugged him warmly. John kissed her and felt her love in the strong embrace she gave her oldest boy. He thought, *What Reverend Hancock says about us Yankees is true for my mother: We have sharp tongues and we're always ready to dispute, but we love deeply. We don't show it outside but it's printed on our hearts.*

"I'm sorry, Mother, to have displeased thee."

"Son John, thy mother is often a fussbudget. Thee's a good son. Sweet sleep and quiet dreams, my dear."

John joined his father and his brother in the back, where they relieved themselves in the men's outhouse. Up the back stairs, then, to the little cubby loft above the kitchen where the boys all slept. John hung his clothes on a wooden peg and climbed into the blankets on his feather-filled pallet. They said their bedtime prayers with their father near, and they were asleep not long after his footsteps left the stairs.

The Blab School

As he awoke in the dark, John remembered with a sinking feeling that it was a school day.

John Adams didn't like school and knew that schoolmaster John Cleverly didn't like having him in his school.

It didn't seem fair. Deacon Adams had not attended school. His mother had taught him to read at home, and he was one of the most respected, wisest men in Braintree. The deacon, in his turn, had taught John to read at home before the boy was five. "What more do I need?" John asked himself. "I can read the Bible and I can read the newspapers. What does a farmer and hunter need with

Master Cleverly's Latin and Greek tedium?"

He rose and dressed in the cool morning. While Peter put his clothes on, John helped Elihu. "There ye are, El. Clothes all on and buttons all done. Ye look like a fine young gentleman this morning. Is it time for our chores?"

Elihu nodded to his big brother solemnly. "Lots of choring to do."

"Well, let's get at it, then."

John was wearing a woolen sweater and helped Elihu into a sweater that was once his own, like everything else that El was wearing. As they came down the back stairs to the kitchen, his mother was fanning the fire into life on the hearth.

"God bless us this day," John greeted his mother.

"Yes, John, and thee especially, Elihu."

"Me 'specially." El nodded.

There was a good deal to do before John could even think about school. Elihu didn't have real chores yet, but he wanted to be included, to be a big boy. In the cool, dark morning outside, under the open woodshed roof, John put five or six sticks of dry kindling into El's arms before he filled his own. "First, kindling for Mother's fire, yes?"

"Kindling first," Elihu agreed, walking importantly ahead of John to the kitchen.

The wind was coming up a bit. The day was cooler and looked cloudy, the kind of uncertain day before a storm that Yankees called "a weathermaker." When John nudged the door latch with his elbow the wind took the door and a great gust rushed into the kitchen.

"Fishes and fowls!" cried Susanna Adams. "You've scattered ashes everywhere, John. Can you not be prudent about the wind, then? Consider, John, consider!"

"Apologies, Mother," John stammered, making sure El was through the door before he closed it with his shoulder. "It's a weathermaker out there."

"Early autumn, early spring," she replied, busy with the corn broom, brushing the ashes into a wooden scoop and dumping them into a tin scuttle. "We'll need every handful of these for soap making." Hardly anything on a Yankee farm went unused.

Outside again, John gave El another half dozen

sticks of kindling while he began to carry logs for the fireplace. Wind through the kitchen door was once again a problem and a notion of how to improve the situation began to form in John's mind.

But first, the livestock. El stayed by the fire in the kitchen and John joined his father in the dairy barn. He forked sweet-smelling hay into Anne's manger as the deacon sat on a low stool with his head against her smooth, brown-and-white side, milking her. The splashing of the milk foaming into the pail was a pleasant little melody.

John began to fork hay into the manger for Henry, one of the plough oxen. "Father?"

"Speak to me, John," the deacon said.

"I am thinking of an invention."

"Yes, good."

"A strong north wind blows too roughly into the kitchen. It scatters ashes and dust. Yet every morning, north wind or not, we must bring in the wood."

"Yes?" The splashing went on.

"I am thinking of fashioning a small door beside the kitchen door. Outside this small door we could build a large box with a large lid. Say, a span wide."

John probably meant his span, as far as his arms would reach spread wide. "Then one could fill up the box from the outside. When mother needed more wood she could open the inner door and pull in dry wood. Is this practical?"

The splashing stopped and Deacon Adams clucked his tongue thoughtfully, his thinking habit. "Ye are a mechanic, John," the deacon said, complimenting him. "For certain, a workable idea. It has many merits. I ask myself if we can take it a step further. What if we combined this box with a larger box? Not so much a box, but a small room at the back of the kitchen with your wood box at one side of it. This would be a room outside the kitchen door, a room for soiled things and pattens." "Pattens" were wooden clogs worn over shoes in the mud. "And this small room would have a door of its own. A body would enter the outer door and close it. Take off pattens or brush off water, then enter the door into the kitchen. No wind would blow in then, would it?"

"No, sir."

The hissing began again. "Think ye, John, these

inventions would make the kitchen snugger and warmer?"

John thought a moment. "I think yes."

"Then this winter thee and I shall build your kitchen-warming invention, John, and we will all benefit. I thank thee, son."

John was more pleased with his father's approval than with anything he could imagine. But the idea was not his alone: "God gave me a mind to think with, Father. Not to use it would be a waste."

Patiently milking Anne, Deacon Adams nodded and chuckled.

While Peter was gathering eggs in the hen house, John scattered dry, cracked corn for the chickens. He drew well water for his mother's kitchen, then drew enough water to mix grain, kitchen peelings, and old turnips for the pigs. He called them to their pen. "Sweee! Sweee! Pigs, pigs! Come along, pigs. Come along Brutus, Zion, William . . . come along Master Cleverly. Come and eat, fat porkers."

"John," his father called from the barn, "are ye being unkind to the schoolmaster or to the pig?" It was his father's gentle way of correcting him for calling the pig, whose name was really Zeno, after his schoolmaster.

"It's a fine pig, Father," he called back, "but I was wicked in slighting the schoolmaster."

"Remember John Cleverly in your prayers, John Adams, so that ye remember your slight of him." His father left the barn with a pail of milk and together they walked to breakfast.

Breakfast was a hearty meal on a Massachusetts farm. Cider, oatmeal with maple syrup, bacon, bread, jam, and tea. But after breakfast it was time to think of school. John walked out the front door and turned right through the stone wall toward the village. He stopped and looked behind him toward the marsh, where he truly wanted to go, then walked on to Master Cleverly's.

School had always been a disappointment to John. It was a droning, slow, boring torture every day. Learning to read from his father had been a good game, but Dame Belcher's school, where Peter still went, had been an awful disappointment!

It had been a "blab" school. Students blabbered

out their lessons all together in a noisy uproar. The little ones read and shouted their lessons from their hornbooks—small wooden paddles with printed alphabets and sayings pasted on them. So that dirty hands would not soil the parchment, flat-pressed, transparent boiled horn was tacked over the words and letters. John remembered many of them still:

> In the burying place may see,
> Graves shorter there than I,
> From death's arrest no age is free,
> Young children too must die.
> My God may such an awful sight,
> Awakening be to me!
> Oh! that by early grace I might
> For death prepared be.

John knew that many children died. Half the children born in Braintree died before they were ten. One out of every three babies died before they were two years old. The Adams family had been lucky.

After hornbooks, John moved on to the *New England Primer,* a small schoolbook that began with letters and syllables and went on to an alphabet in verse, with woodcut pictures. Each letter had a Biblical theme:

A *In ADAM's Fall*
We sinned all.

D *The Deluge drown'd*
The Earth around.

J *JOB feels the Rod,*
Yet blesses GOD.

John had felt like Job at Dame Belcher's. The Devil tested Job's love for God by sending torments and pains. Surely none of them was worse than shouting out his lessons, already stale from repeating them over and over, day by day.

The primer went on from its simple verse alphabet to a more advanced prose alphabet:

✻ ✻ ✻

Better is a little with the fear of the Lord, than great treasures and trouble therewith.

LIARS shall have their part in the lake which burns with fire and brimstone.

Seest thou a man wise in his own conceit, there is more hope of a fool than of him.

John feared his own conceit, his vanity in thinking himself too fine-tempered for the drudgery of school. He thought he must be a very stupid boy to do so badly at school.

He was late to the schoolhouse. He stepped carefully and soundlessly on the wooden porch, opening the door as quietly as he could. Not quietly enough.

"John Adams," Master Cleverly said sourly, "ye are late to school. Perhaps a caning would correct this ill-temper in thee?"

"I ask your pardon, Master Cleverly. My feet were slow upon the road this morning." He hurried to his bench.

The schoolroom was chilly and his friend Edmund Quincy was snuffing with a runny nose. He looked across at John and smiled.

Whack!

Cleverly's thin cane smacked on his desk so quickly and loudly that every boy in the room jumped.

"There is too much social visiting going on in my classroom. I am the master of that classroom, and you young creatures will be strictly obedient to me and to my lessons in this classroom."

Whack!

They all jumped again.

"And now we shall decline the Latin verb *vincus,* to conquer, and each of you will use it in a sentence of your own, beginning with you, John Adams, and going around the room."

John went suddenly blank. He knew the verb, he wanted to speak plainly, but his dissatisfaction at being here in this room crowded in on his mind.

"John Adams!"

Whack!

John blinked his eyes a moment and then said,

Labor omnia vincit. Work conquers all."

Cleverly groaned theatrically. "Too common, too common. It is an old saw out of a young and lazy mouth. Apply yourself, Adams! Go on, next student!"

Cleverly retreated to his chair and pretended to listen, though John was certain that he was not listening, merely passing the time. John heard several mistakes of grammar in the Latin sentences that went unchallenged. He knew that if he had made the same mistakes, Master Cleverly would have humiliated him in front of his friends.

The Latin lesson came to an end. How could Cleverly make the old Romans sound so dull? Were they boring? No, John loved them. They were quicker and brighter than sour John Cleverly.

John put his Latin text away and pulled out *Mathematicks.* His mind was still boiling and bubbling, like a pot on the fire. Yes, he knew the structure of the sentences, knew most of the words, but . . . but . . .

John's inner voice—that dark self that complained and criticized—spoke harshly: *Once again, this is your vanity and arrogance.* John shrugged his shoulders up hard in embarrassment and made a terrible face. This was a habit, the way John Adams reacted to his own shame.

Whack!

Cleverly's cane hit the desk again.

"John Adams, are you sickly, boy? What is that wretched expression for?"

"Beg pardon, Master Cleverly. A passing twinge, a chill."

"A disgusting and ridiculous display, Adams. As disgusting as Quincy's snuffling. Sit ye down, all you disgusting creatures, and let us all get on with our lesson in the advanced arithmetic."

Here was something that Master Cleverly knew and liked: advanced mathematics. When he was teaching this subject, he seemed to forget his cruel barbs and startling whacks. Though he continued to speak, it was almost as if he were speaking to himself. He drew the triangles and circles on the chalkboard carefully, interested in their power to reveal something—but not to his students—he was drawing for himself.

In the weeks to come, John Adams's struggle with Cleverly over the old Romans and the Latin sentences continued and became even more bitter. Yet there was no friction between them when mathematics was the subject on the slate. John was too fascinated by the cleverness of the proofs and by the abstract rhythms of the numbers. Perhaps school wouldn't be so grim?

Then Cleverly decided that the class had gone far enough in mathematics. "The rest," he announced one afternoon, "is beyond your understanding. Higher and purer minds will take delight in the more difficult and more abstract mathematics, not country blockheads like you."

"Sir!" John Adams spoke up.

"What?" Cleverly cried in shock. "What? What is this? You dare to use that tone with me, John Adams? Get thee up here this instant! Lay across that desk, ungrateful puppy!"

In confusion John rose and lay across the desk, grasping the far edge.

Whack!

This time the noise came from the seat of John Adams's trousers, not the desk.

Whack!

Whack!

"There, boy. I hope thee are chastened and humbled. What have ye to say?"

John gritted his teeth. "This, sir. Though I apologize for offending thee, I insist that our minds are not impure and not lacking understanding. The higher mathematics is, sir, within our grasp if you will only . . ."

"Back across that desk, boy!"

John's trousers met the bamboo cane again and again.

The Field

But school didn't darken every day. How could it? There was work to do!

After morning chores one Thursday, Deacon Adams sat at breakfast and blew on his steaming tea. "The corn in the north field prospers," he said, "but so do the Philistine weeds, boys. Let us go among the wicked and smite them, hip and thigh!"

He laughed like a boy. It was his strange sense of humor to see the weeds as the wicked Philistines in the Bible, to be battled with their "swords." After breakfast the deacon, John, and Peter picked up their swords—hoes—in the tool-shed and set off for the fields.

"Why don't we just let the weeds grow, Father?" John asked as they walked.

"Look over there, boys." He pointed to a distant field where a tiny figure was rising and falling, smiting his own Philistines. "There's Jabez Bass working his field. I respect him and he respects me. Jabez's success doesn't depend on my failure, does it?"

"Well, sir, he has the same rain and the same sun, I suppose. A good year for us is a good year for him."

"Yessuh. Jabez lets me farm my fields as I wish. I feel that he should farm his, likewise. It's his field, his chance at profit."

"But unlike our friend Jabez, the weeds are lawless and selfish. Did I plant them? I did not, nossuh. They have planted themselves without my consent. And do they seek our mutual benefit? They do not, nossuh. They seek only their own increase, which must be at my expense. They steal the food and water from under our good corn plants. God forbid, boys, they may come from Weymouth!"

All three giggled. Weymouth was another village

down the coast. Folks from Braintree and Weymouth were friendly rivals in the footraces, jumps, and lifts at the harvest fairs.

They had reached the north cornfield. "These weeds are the enemy. They're the lawless rabble of the vegetable world, boys. Shall we conquer them?"

"Yessuh!" both boys shouted, and they went to their work.

All morning they attacked the Philistine weeds with their swords. Working down the space between two rows, the deacon would hoe up weeds from one side, John and Peter from the other. Now and then they would turn up the bones of menhaden, the oily herring that the deacon and other farmers netted in the spring to fertilize the fields.

"Why do we plant fish?" Peter asked. "They never grow."

"Well, Peter, they don't grow green fish, but they grow green corn," the deacon said. "They make the soil rich, and the corn benefits."

"How did we know to plant fish with the corn?"

The deacon rested on his hoe and stretched his back for a moment. He looked over the fields. "A hundred years ago, old Henry Adams, your great-great-grandfather, came to Braintree. In 1638, that was. And before him came other Puritans here, and Pilgrims down Plymouth way." He gestured to the south.

"Those early folks . . . well, to be charitable, they were city people and knew more about scripture than about keeping themselves alive. They hardly made it, really. More than half of them died. They call those early years 'The Starving Time.' They were lucky, though. They made friends with the Wampanaugs and the Ponkapoags. The Indians taught them to plant the fish with the corn. Taught them a lot about surviving New England winters. They were good friends."

"There weren't very many of them," John said. "We only know a few dozen Ponkapoags."

They were back at hoeing, now, and the deacon said, "There were plenty of Indians then. Sweet and shy they were, as my grandmother remembered them. Most of them died."

"Did we kill them in a battle?" Peter asked.

"No, Peter," the deacon said, "But we brought a

battle to them. They were terribly frail against the sicknesses that came with us. Especially smallpox."

A little chill went through both boys at the mention of the dread disease.

"We lost many to disease, but for every one of our people who died, ten or twenty Indians died, all up and down the coast. Not many left, now."

"That's sad," Peter said.

"I s'pose," the deacon said, stretching his back again, "that a truly Godly man might say everything works according to God's plan. I trust that's the case. But, Peter, I agree with you. The loss of the original people, here, is a great sadness."

Nothing was better for John than working and talking with his father, being outside, smelling the wind and the fresh-opened soil.

It was a big field but the three of them weeded it by midday. They walked back toward the house past their field of potatoes and onions. The deacon reached down and pulled a fine-looking yellow onion.

John asked, "Shall we start on the potatoes after we eat, sir?"

They stopped as their father looked back to the cornfield and examined the potato patch. "No, sir, we will not. I will work at my cobbler's bench, and you two will make yourselves busy at being boys. Go and play with the Braintree Wild Boys on the Common. Weather's warm again. Won't have too many more of these days before it turns. Nossuh."

They came into the kitchen and Susanna Adams cried, "Wipe y'feet! Dusty farmhands, bringing half the field into my kitchen!"

"That we are, woman," the deacon said grinning. "We are as dusty and as hungry a bunch of farmhands as Braintree can offer."

They ate potato soup and thick slices of wheat bread with cheese and thin slices of field-fresh onion. They drank beer. Men, women, and children drank beer because water wasn't healthy. The groundwater was tainted with runoff from cowbarns and outhouses. People who drank well water got sick. Before pasteurization, milk was not safe, either. Fermentation purified beer and wine and hard cider.

One of the best parts of the meal was watching

Susanna shape the crust of three apple pies. The twigs were crackling and snapping in the fireplace oven.

Even with the prospect of school in the back of his mind, life seemed like a constant delight to John Adams. They had the whole, glorious, sunny afternoon to play on the Common, and there would be a golden apple pie after dinner!

The Reed Flats

Deacon Adams and his oldest son sat on rough firkins in the rake shed. John knew what his father wanted to talk about.

"Thee's a good son, John, and have my love. D'ye know that?"

"Yes, sir."

"A good hunting day with the dogs?"

"Yes, sir."

"Was it a day thee were to be in school?"

"Yes, sir."

"And the reason thou weren't in school?"

"Master Cleverly's schoolroom . . ." John began, then faltered. John wanted more than almost anything in the world to please his father. "Master Cleverly . . . I can't hold my interest in what Master Cleverly teaches," he said finally, even though he knew this was not the whole problem.

Deacon Adams shook his head and looked at his big, callused hands. John knew how much importance the deacon gave to learning. He knew how much his father wanted him to attend Harvard College like the Reverend Adams, one of John's uncles. After a long pause, Deacon Adams looked up to John. "What would thee be, boy?"

"A farmer, Father. Like you, a freeholder and a man of the land."

"And of the seasons. And the rains. Or no rains. Or storms. Or wheat rust and cabbage worms. A man of laboring daily with no time for reflection and reading. This is what you'd be, John?"

"Yes, sir. A Braintree farmer."

The deacon shook his head again and looked above them to the shed roof. "Very well, John. Look above you. What d'ye see?"

"I see thatch, Father."

"And what else?"

"Just thatch and ties and pole beams."

"Look more carefully, John, and thee'll see daylight. Be a farmer with me, then. Tomorrow we'll do farmers' work and cut thatch for our outbuildings. See how real farming—not chores and carrying water for the kitchen—suits you."

John and the deacon rose early the next day and ate quickly. Susanna packed them a midday meal of bread and smoked meat and a jug of beer. Before dawn they had milked Anne, fed the livestock, and had hitched the oxen to a wagon. Before full light they were on their way to Penn's Ferry Marsh and the reed flats.

They didn't ride the ox cart but walked beside the oxen. John carried a long ash pole with a tongue of leather fastened to the end. He guided and hurried the oxen with this, tapping their flanks with the pole, occasionally snapping the leather tongue with a crack over their heads.

They tethered the oxen on long tethers in the grass at the marsh edge. They hung everything but their trousers on the wagon and made their way

across the broad flat to the great reed beds. Their bare feet sunk into the thick mud at every step. They moved slowly with their knees bent and their curved sickles held out to the side. The shore breeze was cool and the mud was downright cold. The only thing John wore above his trousers was a length of coiled line and the little leather bag that held his sharpening stone.

The reeds were in shallow water at this tide. Standing knee-deep in the young sunlight, Deacon Adams showed John how to whet the blade of his sickle with a few quick strokes. "A rock or a hard stump will nick the edge, and that'll be a trip to the wagon for filing. Look for a clear swing and keep all thy fingers, John!"

They started into the reed wall, tough and dense. John found that cutting with a sickle required concentration and planning. It wasn't rhythmic and regular, like using the big scythe on grass. At times he sank to his knees in soft patches of marsh mud, and several times he let out a yelp when a crab tried to claim one of his toes with a pincer.

Deacon Adams laughed. "The crabs think thee're sweeter than Master Cleverly thinks thee are, John."

They laid the sickled reeds behind them until the pile grew high. Then they used the cord to bind the shifting stack of hollow grasses into loads as big as themselves but lighter than Elihu and struggled back across the marsh with their loads on their backs. They stacked the big shocks of reed on the wagon, tying layers of them down in succession.

John could no longer feel the crabs and fish and shrimp on his toes. They were numb with cold up to his shins. He was covered with mud to his belly button and his trousers were heavy with salt water. He stubbornly continued beside his father, pushing himself to cut loads just as big and carry them as far and as fast, but he couldn't hoist them high into the wagon. His father helped him to load and tie down.

Come the midday meal, John didn't want to sit down for fear he could not stand up again. But he had to sit; he was so tired! His back was sore and cold. His bottom felt raw and chapped. The drying mud itched and the sweat swam into his eyes and stung them. They ate and returned at once to the reeds.

The distant end of afternoon crawled toward them. Now the mosquitoes plagued John so much that he dabbed marsh mud on his shoulders and the backs of his arms to keep them off.

Finally, the load of reeds was as high as they could tie down. Deacon Adams hitched the oxen to their yoke and they began the walk home. John was limping from stepping on a sharp clamshell in the reed flats. Both the father and son were too filthy to think of putting the rest of their clothes back on. They walked for miles, John just keeping up with his father, using the last of his will and energy.

They stopped at a creek and washed away the black mud.

At the Adams farm, the deacon and John unloaded the high stack of reeds beside the sheds, ready for thatching. The dry reed leaves cut John's hands, and the gritty dust from the reeds made him itch worse than the mud.

As the sun was approaching the horizon, they took off their trousers behind the house and Susanna Adams, clucking over their dirt, poured buckets of water over their heads. They washed with handfuls of soft soap. It seemed to John as if the soap and the water had washed all the starch and stuffings out of him. He sat on a cedar stool by the well, exhausted.

Deacon Adams sat beside him, drying in the breeze.

"How does thee like farming now, John?"

Stubborn John Adams answered pridefully, "Yes, sir, I like it very well." Even as he spoke, he knew it was his vanity speaking. John Adams was one stubborn Yankee.

Deacon Adams, exhausted himself, shook his head and lowered his gaze. "Aye, John, but I don't like it so well. So you shall go to school tomorrow." And that was an end to it.

The Latin School

John was creeping across the marsh with his bow stealthily, he had learned from Hezakiah Squamogg. There was a small flock of geese in one of the marsh creeks. They would paddle out against the incoming tide. Hidden in the grass, his arrow nocked, he waited in the light breeze.

A goose honked, so close it almost startled John out of hiding. He drew his bow slowly and sighted through the grass.

Hiss! Thump!

Hiss! Thump!

John's bow was unstrung and two fine geese hung from the end over his shoulder. He was whistling a tune as he skirted the soft part of the marsh.

There he met a stranger carrying a telescope.

"I wish thee a good day, sir," John called.

"And to thee," the stranger replied. He held up his telescope. "I watched your skill with the bow. Where did you learn to shoot like that?"

"From the Ponkapoags, sir. Mighty hunters." John held out his hand, "I am John Adams, son of Deacon Adams in Braintree, sir."

The stranger didn't speak immediately, then said, "So you're young John Adams. I've heard of thee, young man. My name is Joseph Marsh. I keep a school on t'other side of Braintree, a little ways on toward Weymouth."

Master Marsh didn't seem like a schoolmaster, or at least like any schoolmaster John had met.

"What do you teach at your school, sir?" John asked.

"Why, we teach whatever the intellects of our students will absorb, young Adams. But we stress Greek and Latin in preparation for university. You're a pupil at Master Cleverly's school, are you not?"

"Yes, sir." John tried not to make this admission sound discouraged.

"I've heard tales—just tales mind you, and no reflection on you or the conscientious Master Cleverly—that his classes don't inspire your scholarship?"

"He is a good man," John replied, "and I am certain he is an excellent teacher. The fault is mine."

"Don't be too eager to accept all the burden, Adams. But be certain that you do justice to your mind and not starve it out of spite. No offense, young sir?"

"No offense, Master Marsh."

"Come and see us sometime on the Weymouth road."

"I thank thee, sir."

John and his geese headed for home.

Weeks later, before dinner, Deacon Adams asked John to sit with him in the parlor. He took a folded note out of his vest pocket and held it by a corner, as if he didn't know what to do with it. "Here is a vexed note from Master Cleverly, calling my son a ne'er-do-well and a spiteful, disobedient student. He says that you took one of the mathematical textbooks out of the classroom and kept it at home over the Sabbath. This is true?"

"Yes, sir. I did keep the textbook, but returned it on the Monday following."

"And what did you do with this book, John?"

"Sir, I learned the mathematics that Master Cleverly refused to teach us. He called us country-ants with no understanding."

"And now you have an understanding of these . . . mathematics?"

"Yes, father, I do. And it is a satisfaction to me. There's great order and mystery in the mathematics. I grant that I studied on the Sabbath but it was not work for me. It was seeking for knowledge. Cleverly wants to keep the knowledge for himself. He thinks we . . . he thinks that *I* am unworthy of advanced concepts. I cannot respect the man."

Deacon Adams looked at the note. "But he is thy schoolmaster, John. What think ye of study? Is there worth in it for you? I have hoped there would be."

"Sir, Master Cleverly is careless of our lessons and he is always angry. He is so soured on me that I can never be easy with him or learn anything from him."

"But what shall we do about your studies, John?"

The solution was suddenly and perfectly clear to John. "Father, can we persuade Mr. Joseph Marsh to take me into his school? I will work very hard for him. I have met the man and respect him. I've talked with his students.

"He is no petty tyrant, Father. I will promise you that, with Master Marsh, I will apply myself to my studies. I believe with his help I can master Latin and Greek and the subjects I need to pass the Harvard examinations. With his help and your blessing, I will go to college as soon as I can prepare."

There was a long silence in the parlor. John began again, "Father, I have most of the Latin . . ."

Deacon Adams shook his head, then smiled. "No, John, you've mistaken my silence for objection. I have no objection to any part of what you've said. This," he held up the note from Master Cleverly, "is a peevish and unworthy letter. The man reveals his sour nature here. I have heard much good of

Master Marsh. My silence, John, was not objection but relief. I have feared that thee would not go to Harvard because the love of learning wasn't strong enough in ye. I was wrong. I misjudged you. I ask your pardon."

John Adams stood and put his head on Deacon Adams shoulder. He was near a grown man, he knew, but his father's arms around him still felt wonderful.

John's step was quick. The pace of his walk suddenly struck him as strange: He was actually hurrying to school. This was a change from the way he walked to Cleverly's schoolroom a few months ago! It was a long hike to Master Marsh's school—across Braintree and around the south marsh—but each morning his stride quickened as he looked forward to the business of the day—the business of learning.

The change in how John and his classmates were treated was surprising too. To John Cleverly, pupils were village dullards, a burden to haul wearily toward enlightenment. To Joseph Marsh they were "young citizens," or "young gentlemen," already graced with intelligence, lacking only guidance and experience to become Massachusetts leaders. And, because they would be leaders of the most progressive and modern colony, Master Marsh was confident that they would be leaders of a new society in the New World.

Of course there were no young women in the class. True, young women could be taught to read, but their place in society was not in the rough-and-tumble of daily affairs, politics, business, or law. They were gentler, more refined creatures, to be protected and sheltered. The old Roman and Greek writers were too rough-handed, too bawdy for young women's delicate senses. Young women should certainly read the Bible, and perhaps some novels of romance. They would not need much education. Their later lives would be less eventful, smoother than men's lives, and if they were fortunate they could raise fine children and make a good home for one of those Massachusetts leaders.

John thought a great deal about young women, lately. Something about the respect Master Marsh showed him changed his own view of himself. *And charged up my vanity even more*, that inner voice said to him. *I preen like a peacock in front of girls. I take a vain care with my dancing and singing. But I know how clumsy I must seem!* John shook his head as he crossed one of the half dozen bridges along his walk to school.

"Why am I so full of trouble and arguments?" he asked himself out loud. "I enjoy people, love a crowd—yet I'm truly shy and stiff when folks are around. I'm passionate and loud about nearly every notion that comes into my head—yet I doubt everything I say as soon as I say it. Anyone might mistake me for a bully sometimes, or a persnickety old lady at other times. Outside I'm all bluster and confidence. Inside I'm all doubt. I'm critical of others, but I mope through long, black moods. I'm afraid I'm more like my mother than the deacon." He leaned over the railing and saw himself reflected in the dark water below, and shook his head again. "And worst of all, I think about myself all the time!" That, and the peering, jowly boy looking back up at him, was enough to make him laugh before he went on his way.

"Thee haven't brought thy fowling piece with thee this morning, John Adams," Master Marsh commented cheerfully as John hung his hat and coat by the door.

"Nossuh. More than that, I noticed a speck of rust on the barrel of my best bird gun this morning. Your class has crowded out my bird shooting. The number of birds on the salt flats has increased enormously." His classmates laughed along with Master Marsh.

Mathematics was the morning's first subject, and it was John's favorite. It had a charm for John. The formulas and concepts were difficult to understand at first, like a mysterious story. But they were wonderfully satisfying to grasp and use.

Master Marsh introduced John's class to natural philosophy—science. They learned how numbers affected the world around them: the number of spokes in a wagon wheel, the number of paddles on a water wheel, the number of times a flying bird beat its wings each minute. John began to see the connection between numbers and forces and things: music, the bang and white smoke from his squirrel rifle, the impact of the bullet, the time it took for the sound of thunder to reach him from distant lightning.

In addition to mathematics and science, the young gentlemen studied Latin, Greek, history, and geometry. Master Marsh also taught a skill he considered indispensable to his young leaders: elocution, the art of speaking.

It was a subject that both delighted and frightened John Adams. Sometimes, practicing a speech on the way to or from school, his inner voice would stop his dramatic speaking. He would wince and draw his shoulders up in shame. *Drunkards need rum,* he warned himself, *and I seem to need an audience. My vanity leaps and burns when people are listening, like pouring brandy on a blazing plum pudding. Such wicked delight cannot be moral.* But at other times he contended with that inner voice and knew that there were powerful things he might do with the support of an audience. *If I speak the truth, and lead others to it with the power of my speech, don't I serve truth?*

John practiced gestures and vocal rhythms he

had heard from ministers and political speakers. He tried to use them in his class speeches, but more than once Marsh would call from the back of the room, "No, no, no! The art of elocution does not address the *ears* of your audience, Adams. All the airy tricks of preachers and politicians to make poor words and weak thoughts interesting are false paint and powder. The art of elocution addresses the *minds* of an audience. Real grace of elocution, real skill, is in arranging your beliefs and thoughts in a simple, convincing, natural way."

Deacon Adams returned from a town council meeting late one evening and found John studying by the light of a candle at the kitchen table. He patted his son's shoulder as he passed, and poured them both a mug of hard cider, John's favorite. The deacon sat down at the table with John. "Mr. Marsh has cost me doubly." He smiled as John looked up. "I pay Joseph Marsh for schooling, and now I pay Winfield Talbot for ducks. Nimrod the mighty hunter has become Adams the mighty scholar."

John grinned. "I'll knock down a few ducks on Saturday, if thee hungers for game."

"Studies first, John, studies first. Mr. Marsh tells me your work goes well. I confess that I do not see ye as often as I did when you were only a middling scholar. Ye are bound to these pages. Does Marsh tax you with too much work?"

"No, much worse than that. He tells us to learn what we can. But he thinks so highly of our abilities to learn that we tax ourselves. D'ye remember how hard I ran my hounds after the bobcat that was getting at the chickens?"

"Yessuh. And a good hunt it was."

"That excitement, that running after understanding and new ideas, is what I sometimes feel running through these pages. There's more than one hunt, Father."

Deacon Adams nodded his head as he rubbed his eyes. "Best get some sleep, Johnny. Thee've been working hard."

"I'll come up soon."

"Bless thee, son," Deacon Adams said, and John was comforted by his father's familiar step as he went up the stairs.

The Woodlot

John Adams awoke to a changed world. The mild weather of soft gray skies and brief morning frosts had been blasted away by a rampaging "Northah," a storm whirling down out of the Canadian arctic north, full of snow and spite. The temperature had dropped thirty degrees overnight and the wind had arrived with a fury. John shivered as he looked out the upstairs window.

John leaped back into his bed. "Whoo!" He tried his breath in the cubby attic, and the word became a cloud over his blankets. "Elihu?" he called. "Are you warm enough, El?"

"Cold," El said from under his covers. "El's cold this morning."

"Come over here, then, and warm up," John said.

Little El exploded from the covers as if he'd been waiting for the invitation, and burrowed under John's blankets like a groundhog. A few moments later they were joined by Peter. El, between them, murmured, "Better. John and Peter warm up El."

Later, sitting at the table before steaming oat and barley porridge, Susannah Adams opened the new wood box door and peered in. "If I'm to bake bread and meat f'the Adams family, I'll need a load of faggots for the oven soon. I've seen bettah days for fetching them in, Mr. Adams, but that oven is greedy for 'em."

Deacon Adams turned to John. "What say ye, weather prophet?"

John was flattered. He knew his father was as good a weather predictor as any man in Braintree. But it was Deacon Adams's way to step back and let others shine.

"Fierce as this wind is, I s'pect it'll blow itself out before midday. Yessuh," said John. "Doesn't feel like the snow will stop with it, though. I could get over to the woodlot with the sled and haul back a good lot of faggots."

The deacon nodded his head in agreement and said, "You shu'wah?" drawling the word "sure" out in two syllables. "I'd come along but there's town business."

Susanna snorted again. "And where's the town when we need help thatching or fencing, I ask you. Mr. Adams, you spend yourself too lavishly on this town. It's a losing bargain."

"Mothah'," Deacon Adams voice was just a trifle firmer—he would accept no argument on this point, "no bargain is a loss if it benefits the common good. God gave us increase so's we could help a few less fortunate souls. Some are asked to give from their talents, Mothah'. Ability is responsibility."

"Well, Mr. Adams, I hope and pray you are in the right of it. And that the Adams don't starve while we're feasting the orphan children of Braintree."

Deacon Adams cleared his throat like a bull

huffs before charging, and Susanna Adams shook her head at the stubbornness of her menfolk.

"John, it would be helpful in thee to fetch fuel f'ya mothah', but only when the wind isn't quite so frisky. And mind ye to be back by sundown, yes?"

"Yessuh," John agreed.

John Adams hurried through the snow, his breath pluming ahead of him like a tea kettle's steam. He was dressed in five or six layers of wool and linen. His boots were wrapped in sacking, against the cold, and the sled line was looped around his shoulder.

The Blue Hills rose ghostlike up ahead of him in the snow. A part of Braintree—and of most other New England villages—was its woodlot, the forest that provided what comfort Yankees could wrestle from the winter. Wood and the sun were their only resources for heat. There was some talk that deposits of coal, a kind of burnable rock well-known in England, had been found in the far mountains of Pennsylvania. For Braintree, those burning rocks might as well be in China. Indeed, China was closer: That was just a long sail in a stout Yankee ship, after all, but Pennsylvania was across the mountains!

John heard harness bells and the faint drum of horse hooves coming down the slope toward him. A big, shaggy-coated cob thumped around a stand of maples and two of the Black Burdocks shouted a greeting from the sledge seat. Old Ben Burdock, the patriarch, pulled up beside John.

"How d'ye do this warm summah day?" the tiny old fellow asked.

"Mr. Burdock," John greeted him from behind the muffler wound around his mouth and nose, "It's John Adams, sir. God bless us on such a day, sir."

The old man, his face sooty from his work, laughed, and his grandson Nate, just as sooty, called, "Howdy, Johnny!"

They were a family of charcoal burners who lived up here beside their mounds. They burned great ricks of wood slowly, covered by mounds of earth away from the air. Day and night they tended their mounds, opening the vents with rocks and leaves or closing them down. After days or even weeks they dug open the mound and brought out the precious charcoal. Everyone needed charcoal.

It was the only thing that made enough heat to soften iron for the blacksmith's work. Whiskey and rum distillers, like some of John's uncles, filtered their product through crushed charcoal. Of course the little powder mill needed charcoal, along with sulfur and saltpeter, for making gunpowder.

"Come up to the Hills to fetch some snow, Johnny?" Ben Burdock asked with a cackle. He had climbed down and was checking his horse's hooves with a little iron pick for ice balls that could bruise its tender inner-hooves.

"Yes, sir. The deacon just wasn't satisfied with the quality of the snow down there by the marsh. 'Get ye up in the hills and bring me back some fancy snow,' he said to me."

Ben Burdock cackled again as he mounted the seat of his sleigh. He reached under the seat and fiddled with a fold of paper. "Here, Johnny," he said, "f'your drawin's n'such." He gave John half a dozen sticks of straight vine charcoal, the very best drawing tool.

John took them with a grin under his muffler. "Bless you, Mr. Benjamin Burdock. I'll bring thee a squirrel when they're out foraging, again."

"No such a thing, Johnny!" Ben cried happily. "You just keep warm, now. Y'lookin' f'oven faggots?"

"Yes, sir."

"Good pile of brush by a felled oak up the slope, here, 'bout half a mile on. You take care of widah-makahs, heah?"

Widow makers were dead limbs that hung in trees and fell without warning. More than one Braintree forager had been injured, even killed, by a dead limb.

"Yessuh," John said, "and I thank you most respectfully, sir."

"You betcha'," Ben said, and chirruped up his horse.

The sound of horse hooves and sledge runners and harness bells faded fast in the snow. After the bells there was just a soft hiss of snow falling through the brittle branches of the forest.

John continued up the hill and found the fallen oak. He broke off dry branches and broke them into smaller bundles of twigs and stacked them tightly on his sled.

Now he was hurrying to be home by sundown.

On another night the darkness wouldn't have troubled him. He knew the roads and woods and fields as well as anyone in Braintree. But the Sabbath day began at Saturday's sundown, and after sundown no work was to be done, no play, no profit, no traveling, no hunting. It was in the scriptures: Keep the Sabbath holy.

He was unloading the wood into the new wood box as the sun was setting. The deacon and Peter came out to help him finish up while his mother complained from inside the house. She opened the new wood box door to comment, "Thee should have been here in the good light, lazy John. Thy father will catch his death out there helping you stay ahead of the sun!" The door slammed shut.

The three unloaded the sled in silence.

The door opened again, "And supper ready this very moment!" Slam.

They continued to unload. At last Deacon Adams commented, "Nice load of wood, John. Must have been a weary pull across the flats?"

"Not bad, sir."

The wood box door opened again, but before Susanna Adams could speak, the deacon's huge voice set the woodbox trembling. "Woman! We're finished out here! Close the door and keep the warm in! We'll join ye in a moment more!"

Peter stifled a snicker and the deacon thumped his head with a knuckle. "Respect y'mothah, Peter! She's a good woman and she watches out for us Adams fellahs."

No snickers but all three grinned in the coming dark.

Susanna Adams's temper was obvious. So was the difference between her words and her actions. Her talk was all nettle and thorn, but her house was all softness and generosity. As they walked inside, John was certain that the smell of his mother's roasted chicken with herbs and rice was certainly what angels smelled when they flew back into heaven from this wicked New England winter.

Susanna Adams was running late too, and was trying to finish up her slow-cooking Sabbath dinner before the light was completely gone, stirring another onion, another spoonful of molasses and a handful of herbs into the simmering pot of beans hung to the side of the fire.

"Cut the bread, Mr. Adams, and get on to eating without me."

"No, Susanna. We will not. Thee are the heart of this family, woman, and we can't bless the food without thy help."

"Mr. Adams, I have my work to finish."

"God's beans will wait long enough for thee to catch thy breath, wife. Sit with your family."

"Sit! Sit, by El, Mama!" cried Elihu. The deacon rose and pulled out Susanna's chair with elaborate politeness.

"A bunch of baby boys!" she muttered under her breath, but John could see that she was pleased that they wanted her with them so much.

The deacon blessed the food and they set to their meal. The Sabbath had begun.

The Meeting

Sabbath morning, the snow had stopped and the bell's voice had a sharp edge in the cold air. When the Adams family heard the bell they left their breakfast tea and pulled on their sweaters, then their coats, then their long cloaks. Deacon Adams folded blankets and gave them to John and Peter. Susanna Adams filled the pierced tin footstove with coals from the fire, then bundled little Elihu so completely that he could hardly walk.

And now the distant drum began to beat. The Adams family walked out the door, the cold snow squeaking underfoot. They moved toward the meeting house on the Commons in a sturdy row:

Deacon Adams, Susanna Adams, Peter Adams, John Adams and, in the wood-sled pulled by his big brother John, looking twice his size in winter wraps, sat Elihu Adams humming to himself.

They assembled outside the meeting house on snow packed down by passing sleighs and sledges. Standing at the side with the wives and children and servants, John Adams saw the structure of New England government laid out in miniature, as clearly as pieces on the chessboard.

The men of Braintree formed up in militia columns. Braintree had begun in the real wilderness a hundred years before, and was shaped by its church. The Puritan families that left England for the sake of their beliefs became Braintree. Church and village were one. The officials of the church were the officials of the town government: the elders were the selectmen managing town business; the deacons were wardens seeing to town laws. The drumbeat and the marks of military rank among the deacons and elders reminded John that the church was also a miniature army pledged to defend the wilderness village from Iroquois warriors and coastal pirates. They had only recently stopped marching into the meeting house with their loaded flintlock rifles.

The congregation marched through the meeting house door in order: Reverend Hancock, the elders, the deacons, the deaconess, and the lay members following them. Men filed into one side of the ground-floor pews, women into the other. As a deacon John Adams's father sat directly before the pulpit. John, with the other children, the servants, and the few black slaves in Braintree, climbed narrow stairs to the gallery. John spread blankets over Elihu's and Peter's knees to make a snug tent for the footstove's heat. He looked down on the plain, bright room, seeing mostly the broad hats of the men and the smaller hats of the women. The windows were big but undecorated. No stained glass, fancy curtains, carvings, or candlesticks. Gold and decoration was part of the old corrupt church of Rome.

This geometric order was part of the Puritan church. And the church was based on one essential idea: Nothing stood between a person's mind and God—neither priest, preacher, pope, nor saint.

Each man and woman was responsible for interpreting God through the scriptures. The "purified" church stripped away the traditions and ritual of the "old" church. They were a village of independent minds, drawn together as a congregation.

John thought of the town meetings held in this same building. A fair lot of independent minds that was. These Puritans were as passionate and independent in their political views as in their religion. At town meetings every citizen had a right to speak up on the town's management, and it seemed to John that every citizen had a different notion of how to get things done. The selectmen of Braintree had to make an ordinance against standing on the pews and shouting. It surprised John that after the shouting, the hot arguments, and the fiercely held views of a town meeting, the citizens of Braintree left the building without battering one another. But the vote—one vote for every household—seemed to soothe and satisfy them. They filed out with a sound idea of the town's plans.

The drum fell silent, the bell stopped its pealing, and the congregation stopped their neighborly chatter. Reverend Hancock stepped up to his pulpit and raised his arms. The entire congregation rose and raised their arms to heaven for the prayer.

Reverend Hancock did not read his prayer. He may have thought about his prayer and his sermon through the week, but Puritans valued what was in the heart, so he spoke what was within him. John admired his skill with the language, the ability to speak clearly and intelligently to the whole village. Everyone echoed his "Amen," and sat down. John rearranged the blankets.

"The scripture for this morning," Reverend Hancock announced, "is from Matthew, chapter twenty-two, verses seventeen through twenty-two." He opened the big pulpit Bible—the simple-language translation, rather than the flowery King James translation—and read:

"Tell us your opinion, then. Is it permissible to pay taxes to Caesar or not?"

But Jesus was aware of their malice and replied, "You hypocrites! Why do you set this trap for me? Let me see the money you pay the tax with."

They handed him a denarius, *and he said,*
"Whose head is this? Whose name?"

"Caesar's," they replied.

He then said to them, "Very well, give back to
Caesar what belongs to Caesar—and to God what
belongs to God." This reply took them by surprise,
and they left him alone and went away.

Reverend Hancock descended from the pulpit
and Deacon William Bass stood. There were no
hymn books, no music—and certainly nothing as
popish as an organ! Just the strong, true voice of
William Bass singing the first two verses of the
Hundredth Psalm:

Praise God, all the earth,
Serve God gladly,
Come into His presence with songs of joy!

Everyone knew the tune and sang back. After
the first part, Bass would "line" the psalm—remind
everyone of the words by speaking quickly between
phrases. Puritans liked to sing. They liked to dance

and laugh too. They were serious about ideas but they weren't sour, solemn folks.

The singing warmed everyone up, which was a good thing. The temperature in the meeting house was below freezing. Reverend Hancock trudged up the steps to the pulpit again, to deliver the first part of his Sabbath sermon. John tucked the blankets in around Peter and Elihu, because a proper sermon could last two or three hours. For John, listening carefully to the argument and to Reverend Hancock's skill in delivering it, the time went quickly.

"The wicked Pharisees asked Jesus if it was permissible to pay a tax to Rome. And we ask ourselves, so far from Mother England, is it permissible . . . is it proper . . . is it moral to pay a tax to that distant authority?"

Reverend Hancock was aware that his sermons were not just moral lessons, but Braintree's main entertainment. This sermon would be a topic of conversation all week long in the village, up in Roxbury, and down in Weymouth, so Hancock used all his skill in presenting it.

"Where is the dividing line between Caesar's rights, and the rights of Braintree?" he asked. In this first part of the sermon, the line was not clear.

Just before noon, the Reverend Hancock reached a dramatic point in his thoughts and let the questions hang in the frosty air. He nodded to the deacons and descended to the church floor to arrange the sacraments of bread and wine for Communion. The frozen cubes of bread rattled like stones in the pewter Communion plate.

Susanna Adams rekindled the fire on the Adams hearth and the heat was wonderfully welcome. The Adams and their guests took off a few layers of their winter clothing. They set their boots at a respectful distance from the fire and toasted their wool-socked feet in front of the hearth.

The deacon brought out a small keg of good Adams beer, brewed by his brother. The malt that made it was toasted in the malt house built in 1640 by the first American Adams, Henry, who had been a maltster in England.

Some folks on the edges of Braintree couldn't

return to their homes for Sabbath supper between the morning and afternoon services. In the winters they ate with village families, and in the summers they hosted picnics for these families from their wagons on the commons. It was a time for catching up, sharing news and recipes, planning summer building and barn-raisings. Before the fire was a grand place to discuss the sermon or politics.

This Sabbath, John's great-aunt was visiting from Charlestown, across the Charles River from Boston. She brought her son, Sam Adams. Sam was older than John, in his fourth year at Harvard College in Cambridge.

"How be ye, Johnny?" Sam asked.

"Very well, sir."

"Call me Sam. I'm your cousin, after all," he said with a smile.

"Sam, then. Tell me, Sam, are you studying to be a minister at Harvard, like Uncle Joseph?"

Sam shook his big head and smiled again. "No, Johnny, I'm not the stuff ministers are made from. Too rough and scratchy for such fine use as that."

John didn't quite know what Harvard taught

beside religion. The deacon wanted him to attend Harvard and become a minister like Uncle Joseph. "What do you study, then, if I'm not prying."

"Not a bit, no. What am I studying?" Sam Adams slouched back in his chair, looking more like a shaggy, well-fed dog than a promising Harvard student. "Well, some of my teachers say I'm studying to undermine the authority of the Massachusetts Supreme Magistrate. I'm writing a thesis on where loyalty lies, John: Does it lie with the authority of a magistrate, or with the common good? What do you think?"

"About undermining authority?"

"No. About being loyal to authority or the common good."

John thought hard for a moment.

"Don't strain y'self, Johnny," Sam said.

Finally, John answered, "I'm not worldly enough to say, cousin. Here in Braintree, it seems to me that authority *is* the common good. Authority is John Quincy and my father and William Bass and others like them. I don't think they could do anything against the common good."

Sam nodded, biting off a chew of twisted black tobacco and offering it to John, who had been chewing since he was eight. Sam chewed for a time. He shook his head, spat, and said, "Nossuh. I don't think they could, either. It's not in them. But my point is that all men aren't as ethical or as smart as John Quincy and Deacon Adams. Nossuh. And when push comes to shove, where will good men stand?"

"Will push come to shove anytime soon, Sam?"

Sam chewed reflectively. He spat into the fire and took a deep swallow of Adams ale. "Dunno." he said.

The traditional Sabbath dinner was on the table. Beans slow-simmered with smoked pork fat, rain water, mustard seed, and molasses in a big, black pot. Bread, butter, jam, beer, and an apple pie for dessert. Deacon Adams blessed the food and the folks who were about to eat it. Then the table was jolly with the sound of pewter spoons on stoneware plates, the buzz of talk, and laughter.

The sermon's second half for the afternoon went on to question the morning's scripture reading.

What was due to Caesar? What was due to God? John thought about what Sam Adams was writing about at Harvard. He was glad Sam was listening to this sermon. Or had he purposely come to hear it? Was this a question being asked in other meeting houses in Massachusetts?

Reverend Hancock finished his sermon with a question in the air. "Each man," he said, "must answer his own Pharisees. We will all be asked to decide between Caesar and God. But will we be aware that the Pharisees have laid a trap for us? The trap is in the question. The answer is neither "yay" nor "nay." Neither Caesar nor God. The true answer is in perceiving where moral truth and political truth meet."

He descended from the pulpit. John noticed many of the Braintree men nodding. Yes, this would be discussed all week long, perhaps longer.

The deacons passed the pewter offering plate. The congregation's tithes were collected and blessed, and again Hancock stepped up to the pulpit for the prophesy.

This was not a prophesy of the future. Seeing

into the future was black magic, not a part of the church. Prophesy was relating the scripture, written long ago, to the understanding of the church in 1741, and to the lives of the congregation. Hancock reread the scripture about the Pharisees and Jesus and the *denarius* with Caesar's face on it. He closed the Bible and addressed the congregation. "What does this scripture foretell in your lives? How does this passage affect you?"

The meeting house was silent for a long time. This was normal. No one would speak until the spirit spoke within him or her. Finally, John's Uncle Peter stood and spoke clearly, the cold air frosting with his speech, "I make spirits. It's the best way to transport and profit from my grain. It is healthy and useful for the common good that I make good spirits. Yet King George and Parliament want a tax paid for every barrel of spirits I ship out of Boston. And the paper for Inky Stafford's press, which enlightens and informs us, is shipped with a tax due to King George. And Will Wallace pays George a tax on the tin from which he makes our lanterns and footstoves. Where does the money go? Who legislated the tax? Were we asked if it was a proper tax? How are we to decide where the boundary between God and Caesar lies when we don't understand the reasons?"

Other men and a few women rose and commented on the scripture. Reverend Hancock corrected them in the meaning of the passage but was otherwise only a referee for an open discussion about God, politics, taxes, King George, and Braintree, Massachusetts.

John Adams wondered if the same debates went on in far lands. He doubted it. He'd heard visitors to Massachusetts say that only Yankees argued so much, and it was a blessing there weren't that many Yankees.

After prayer and blessing, the deaconess walked to the pulpit to discuss church business. "I fear," Widow Burgess said, "that there is a dangerous sickness among us. A calenture and flux that has struck many of our older friends. It took the Widow Bass from us last night. I came this morning from the sickbed of Hops Bradley, who is very poorly."

Hops Bradley with the calenture and flux! John's heart faltered. A fever and diarrhea were hard on an old man. He was so full of knowledge and stories!

"I ask thee to care well for thy parents and older friends with a good purge, camphor bags, and garlic wreaths."

There was another blessing and the congregation filed out of the church in order, pastor and deacons first. Outside in the snow, the villagers shook hands, embraced and blessed one another, and returned to their homes for more scripture and discussion. The Adamses walked somberly toward home.

At the corner of the Commons, John spoke, "I know it is the Sabbath. I would not be a-visiting. But may I go to wish well to Hops Bradley?"

Susanna Adams hugged her boy and took the sled rope from him. Deacon Adams said, "Thee are not visiting but comforting, John, and that's God's Sabbath work for sure."

John watched them go on toward the marsh, then ran toward Hops Bradley's cottage.

The Long Road

"Very well, John Adams. Can you translate these lines of Cicero from the Latin for us?"

"I can, sir:

Nothing can be more disgraceful than to be at war with him with him whom you have lived on terms of friendship."

"And the next line?"

"Yes, sir:

He removes the greatest ornament of friendship, who takes away from it respect."

Master Marsh drummed with his knuckle on his desktop, and John's fellow students drummed on theirs. It was a kind of applause and it made John very happy.

"Excellent, Adams. The rest of you may take Mr. Adams as a model for your studies. He has not only found the meaning of a few words, but the meaning out of old Cicero's heart. Take this old Roman to you as a wise friend. And now it is time to make your way home, young gentlemen. I will see thee next Monday at our usual time."

There was a rumble of desktops and chairs, books and papers, and Master Marsh motioned for John to sit beside his desk, to stay a while.

When most of the students had gone from the room, he balanced a quill pen across his fingertip, sighting along it. "What think ye, John Adams?"

"Of what, Master Marsh?"

"Are ye ready for the examinations in Cambridge?"

It was rare for John to be speechless. Usually he had too many words. But now he struggled. "Sir . . . the Greek is not strong . . . I know my, . . ." and after stammering a few times, gave up.

Marsh continued, "Thee are prepared, Adams. Whether ye believe this or not, thee are prepared. With thy consent and thy father's I'll write to the masters at Harvard Yard and ask them to examine our Braintree bumpkin, to see if he is a Harvard man."

"But Master Marsh . . ."

"Calm thyself, Adams. This is what we have been working toward for a year and more. I know it has affected thy duck hunting and thy fishing . . ."

John grinned and nodded.

". . . but in a good cause. I have confidence in thee. Truly."

"Will ye come with me to Harvard, sir?"

Marsh thought a bit. "I would be willing, for myself, to go. But for thy sake I'll let thee get up to Cambridge alone. Better so. This is the great journey of thy life, Adams. Reach for it, begin it."

In his sixteen years, John Adams had walked up to Boston, down to Plymouth, and Westward into the Blue Hills and the forests beyond. But the walk to Cambridge was the longest, loneliest walk he could remember.

He had counted on Master Marsh to walk with him, to present him to Harvard. Marsh should have made introductions, smoothed the way with a flattering word about "our fine Mr. Adams, our scholar, our lover of Pliny and Horace and Homer."

But Marsh knew John Adams. He knew the contradictions that lived inside him: vain, confident, and even overbearing on Tuesday; on Wednesday, deeply suspicious of his own worth, shrinking from attention, fearing comparison with others. Marsh was a good teacher. He meant to shape young leaders. He felt that sometimes the only way to help a boy was to step back and let him sink or swim on his own.

John was miserable.

It was, indeed, a miserable day: rainy, breezy, cold. He'd set out at first light. His long wool cloak was wet and heavy and flapping around his shins, threatening to trip him.

What a cruel and miserable trick to play! Hadn't

he worked his best for Master Marsh? Hadn't he studied hard and stretched his mind for every subject put before him? Didn't he deserve better than this, walking alone to meet famous scholars he had never seen? What would they think of this country boy wearing his father's hand-me-down hat and homespun wool cloak?

They would see instantly that he was a Swamp Yankee, a marsh boy with ideas above his place in life. They might be polite at first. But the awful probability was that the great men would start to snicker behind their hands: "Look at the little Yankee reed clipper! Isn't he a rural gem? Isn't he simply the silliest hayseed we have seen in years? Where do they get these farm boys? How do they convince them that they might actually attend the oldest and most respected university in the Colonies? Pathetic!"

John trudged on, trying to miss at least some of the puddles in the road.

It would be humiliating. "Very well, then," John announced to the rain, "let them try to humiliate me. They will not flummox John Adams. Let them try their high and mighty ways with a real Swamp Yankee and see how far it gets them. Call me a naive farm boy, will you? I'll show ye!"

He walked north with the great marshes on his right, the sea across them. Occasionally, he could hear the boom of surf. It was about eighteen miles to Cambridge. He crossed the Neponset River and went on to Dorchester. He turned inland, there, for four miles until he reached Roxbury. The country was mostly flat, with stone outcroppings. There was standing water in the low fields. None of the towns were any bigger than Braintree—two or three cobbled streets and shops, then he was through them and moving into broad, lonely fields. A few wagons passed him going south, a coach splashed him as it hurried past going north. Riders passed in both directions, their horse's hides slick in the rain and their hats pulled low over their eyes.

After Roxbury he crossed the Muddy River and skirted the Mud Town Fens. The road began to take him north again, past Cedar Swamp on the south side of the Charles River. About three miles past the Cedar Swamp, he reached the bridge across the Charles River. A clock chime told him it was ten thirty. He would be on time.

He crossed over the bridge, past the town dock. Even in the rain there was lively river trade on the Charles; rowed wherries poled, flat-bottomed scows moved up and down the stream with barrels of things and bales of other things, all wet. He trudged up to the square.

In 1751, Cambridge, Massachusetts, was just another small village, no larger than Braintree. It had a Puritan meeting house, an Anglican church, a few wealthy homes and several outlying farms. Just off the village square stood the brick buildings around Harvard Yard. Like the other villages John had passed through, pigs, dogs, and ducks used the streets along with people and horses. The mud in the streets was deep and fragrant, mixed with the droppings of animals and the run-off from the public "necessaries," outhouses on the streets. John used one of these necessaries before he entered Harvard Yard. He located the building in which his appointment was scheduled. A kindly porter— something like a cross between and janitor and a butler—hung his wet cloak near a stove and pointed him to a room with a small mirror where he could tidy himself before he entered the interview room.

John combed and retied his hair behind his head with a formal black ribbon. He tried to smile at himself in the mirror. The smile looked more like fright than happiness. All his resolve that the high and mighty scholars would not flummox John Adams . . . gone. He heard the university clock strike eleven, then hurried out and up the stairs.

Education was essential to the Puritans. If each person had the responsibility to understand and interpret God, the scriptures, and the world for himself, then he needed a good education. Setting up a university was one of their first priorities. Harvard College was founded in 1636 in the "New Towne" across the Charles from Boston. Because Cambridge was the most famous university town in England, they renamed New Towne to become Cambridge.

John knocked on the door with a trembling hand.

"Come in, please."

John opened the door and made a quick bow.

He found himself at the end of a long, polished table. Four amiable-looking men, well-dressed, stood and bowed back. They smiled calmly, but John's heart was banging so hard they could surely hear it! They looked at him sweetly but with a question in the air: He was . . . ?

"Yes! Yes, sirs. May I present myself to you: John Adams, of Braintree. Of the Braintree Adamses. In Braintree."

They nodded as if they were quite accustomed to young country gentlemen making fools of themselves.

"I've come for the examination. To Harvard. To be admitted. To study."

John wanted to sink into the floor.

"Mr. Adams, we've been expecting you," said a great fat man with a jowly, dinner-loving face. "Good day and bless you, young man. I am President Holyoke. Your teacher, Master Joseph Marsh, has written to us about you and your qualifications. We are happy you have come to visit us. Before I ask you to sit and talk, allow me the honor of naming Tutor Henry Flynt—the boys call him Father Flynt because he is old and wise." The four men chuckled to one another. "This is Tutor Belcher Hancock and Tutor Joseph Mayhew." They all bowed.

"Please, Mr. Adams, take a seat and let us chat about your needs. You have had a long journey this morning?"

"Yes, sir, from Braintree."

"Ah, yes. Home of the famous Braintree Adamses, in Braintree."

Holyoke gave John a smile to show that he was teasing him, not making fun. John's heart was only hammering now, no longer thundering.

"With the letter that Mr. Marsh has sent to us, and the letter from your father . . . Deacon John Adams?" He held up a paper. "Yes, Deacon Adams . . . what we will require additionally is that you provide us with some notion of your aptitude for the Latin. Perhaps you will be so good as to sit with Mr. Mayhew and translate the passages we have made out for you on this sheet."

John took the sheet and his heart stopped. It might never start beating again. He would die here in the Harvard office. The passage was long, complicated, and many of the words were a complete mystery to him! He would never enter Harvard!

Mr. Mayhew stood. "Mr. Adams, are you well?" he asked with genuine worry in his voice.

"Yes, sir," John replied, feeling truly terrible.

"Good, then. Let's step across the hall and find a good working table, shall we?" He was a kind man, but it wouldn't do John any good. The country bumpkin was trapped, skinned, and tanned.

John sat down at a cherry wood desk. Mayhew bustled about, laying out quills, ink, paper, and blotting sand in a pewter shaker.

"Now the object of our exercise, Mr. Adams, is to translate these passages of Latin text into grammatical English. Simple enough, yes?"

John made a muffled groan.

"I'm sorry, I didn't understand your question," Mayhew said as he laid two thick books beside John's papers—a Latin dictionary and a book on Roman grammar.

"You had a question, Mr. Adams?"

John looked at the books, amazed. "I'm permitted to use these books, Mr. Mayhew?"

"Yes, of course, Adams. The text we've provided for translation is quite complex. We wouldn't expect you to know the entire Latin grammar and vocabulary completely by rote, would we? No, no, our job is not to fill minds up with words and facts. Harvard teaches young men to seek the *truth* in words and facts. *Veritas,* Mr. Adams, that is the motto of Harvard University. That's a word you probably know by heart."

"Yes, sir," John replied, and confidence was trickling back into him, "it means 'truth,' sir. And a good motto it is."

The walk back to Braintree was a happy jaunt. The wind was at his back, the rain had blown itself out, and his step was as light as a colt's. He had made his life's longest journey so far, and at the end of it he had peeked through a wonderful door of knowledge and discovery. John Adams blessed each person on the road. He was carrying a shining gift: Deacon Adams's son would be a minister with a Harvard education.

The Yard

Mr. John Adams of Harvard University strode across the Yard.

"G'day to ye, Cousin Webb," he called out. His cousin, Nathan Webb, was playing ball with Moses Hemmenway and David Sewall.

"Johnny," they shouted back, "will ye sing with us tonight at supper? At the Wentworth's in Boston? It's a meal, Johnny." They grinned. If there was a meal, that tough little butterball John Adams would be there.

"Yessuh!" John replied. "I'll take the ferry! After chapel!"

He started up the stairs to his room and his

books. There was little else in the room—a bed, a chamberpot under it, a desk with a chair, a tin spittoon, candles, pegs for John's few pieces of clothing, a fireplace with a few sticks of wood. There was a rack for John's own pewter plate, mug, spoon, and his sharp steel knife. But there were also shelves of treasures: John's books. He loved books with an almost dangerous delight. It was rare to see John Adams without a book.

His wealthy friends called John's room "Spartan." Many of their families were wealthy merchants in Boston. John had dined with them in splendor under silver chandeliers with dozens of candles. But this plain room suited him. *Curious*, he thought to himself as he laid out his paper and quills. *This is nothing like the marsh, Braintree, the ocean. And yet I can't imagine being without so many friends, the lectures and laboratory experiments, the news and the discussions. The atmosphere around my head seems to crackle with fire here, with imagination, wit, and talk. So different. But so comfortable.* He knew that he would take this excitement of the mind back to his marsh or wherever he went.

His friend John Hancock's room was always warm: a fire on the hearth, Persian rugs on the floor, English oak furniture covered in French tapestry with boxes of the finest quality candles. Like other wealthy students, Hancock "ate out" at Brandish's Tavern. His shirts and linens were sent across to Boston to be laundered and pressed.

John Adams liked John Hancock without envy. Adams loved good food but he was satisfied with "commons," the university meals. He knew how Deacon Adams pinched pennies to keep him at Harvard. John and his father were partners in the deacon's dream of education.

The days were long at Harvard. John rose at five, emptied his chamberpot, and dressed for the day. Morning prayers and scripture reading were at six in the chapel. John fetched breakfast—bread and beer—from the kitchen after chapel. He ate it in his own room on his pewter plate, adding some of Susanna Adam's plum jam.

At eight o'clock the day's lecture was given. Students discussed the lecture and studied its subject until a quick lunch at noon—bread with beef or mutton, and beer or hard cider, John's favorite. After lunch, more discussion, study, and writing until evening prayers at five o'clock.

Supper was at six, a more leisurely and more talkative meal in the students' common room. During the week, they ate beef or mutton and bread, plus apple or peach pie. The best treat after a meal, though, was hasty pudding. This New England specialty was made with corn meal and wheat flour, milk, butter, eggs, molasses, nutmeg, and cinnamon, and was boiled in a tightly tied sack. Served steaming hot with cream, there was nothing like it.

At nine in the evening, university rules insisted that all candles be out and the students be asleep. The rules forbade the students from skating on the Charles or firing pistols in the Yard without permission. Rudeness at meals, profaning the Sabbath by idle walking, and opening any door with a picklock were also forbidden. Students were not allowed to wear "indecent clothes or women's clothes," and were required to wear cloaks, coats, or their black student gowns outside the Yard. No lying, buying or selling hard liquor, or public ill behavior was tolerated.

Saturday, President Holyoke lectured on theology and Christian dogma, requiring the students to memorize, recite, and analyze scripture. On that day, the dinner was salt cod.

John and his fellows had no days off. No lectures were held on Sunday, but it was spent studying scripture and attending church. The school was closed for only six weeks a year. The business of Harvard education was serious and strenuous.

John Adams was a good student, careful with a shilling, and never extravagant, but he was never far from fun. There were singing clubs, ball clubs, and debating societies in the evening. There were reading groups, in which students and their guests read the latest stories, novels, and even plays to one another. His friends thought John was a dramatic reader.

And there were girls. The young ladies of Boston and Cambridge looked on Harvard as the choicest orchard from which to pluck their future husbands, for they would surely be the successful men of Massachusetts. John Adams loved the company of Boston women—so genteel, well-spoken, and self-assured. He was a great flirt and an elegant dancer, short and round but bubbling with charm. John was in demand as a guest at dinner parties, balls, and play parties.

He still had his bouts of melancholy. His self-doubts were always with him. He longed, sometimes, to return to his marsh and dogs and guns, but when he did return home for the short summer break he was often eager to get back to Harvard Yard. Susanna Adams's fits of rage and her black depressions dismayed him. His father was forever bringing the poor and broken of Braintree into their house. John wrote in a journal, "My mother frets, squibs, scolds, rages, and raves. Passion, accident, freak, and humor govern this house. It is devoid of cool reasoning."

But as comfortable and exciting as his years at Harvard were, John knew they were only a passage between his childhood and the adult world of large deeds and hard choices.

One of his most difficult choices began to haunt

him. Deacon Adams wanted his son to become a minister. But John was realizing that he didn't have a minister's personality. He remained a stoutly moral Puritan but he was persuaded that President Holyoke was right: "Ministers or pastors should have no hand in making any laws with regard to the spiritual affairs of their people. Every man therefore is to judge for himself in these things."

The year 1750 was a time when the world was unsticking itself from the ancient mud of feudalism. That antique system bound families and their little plots of land to the service of their "noble" lords and landowners. The American colonies, with seemingly unlimited land and resources, resisted the old notion of serfs and nobles. A great social upheaval was coming. Science was part of that intellectual and moral earthquake, and politics followed close behind. Harvard was at the cutting edge of a new age in a new world.

New principles of science were being discovered every day, some of them at Harvard. John was fascinated by the lectures Professor John Winthrop gave in mathematics, science and astronomy.

118

Winthrop had read his celebrated paper on Haley's Comet to the Royal Society in London. He was a friend of the most famous man in the Colonies, the scientist and inventor Benjamin Franklin. John Adams wanted to follow Winthrop into the mysteries of the universe!

Winthrop taught science, Judah Monis taught Hebrew. Four tutors taught all the other subjects. John's tutor was Joseph Mayhew, the kindly man who had given him his entrance examination. One of John's favorite subjects with Mayhew was rhetoric, the study of speaking and writing persuasively. He was now convinced that skill in oratory could be a powerful force for good. Declamations on assigned topics were given each month and John excelled in the simple elegance of his prose and the forcefulness of his speeches. He wanted to become a writer of essays and pamphlets.

John became interested in medicine. Physicians thought they were now certain of the body's functions and how they could be treated: by balancing the four *humors* of the body (blood, phlegm, black bile, and yellow bile), and by observing and reinforcing the tone of the body's blood, veins, and nerves. What a gift it would be to heal the sick with bleeding, purging, blistering, and all the other medical tools! John wanted to become a physician.

During commencement in 1755, John Adams stood before his parents, his fellow students, former graduates of Harvard, and his teachers to speak his thesis in Latin, still used by learned men to overcome national language barriers. He was presented with a diploma written on a sheepskin parchment, and became a Braintree town hero.

But what would he become? He had too many interests, too many possible directions. He remembered cutting thatch on the reed flats, and his father's urgent question: "What would you be?" He had not a clue.

The Schoolhouse

John Adams was hiding. This time there were no ducks. Snagged by indecision—"What would ye be?"—he hid himself from almost everything he knew.

His commencement speech at Harvard was so impressive that he was immediately offered a position that suited an educated young man without direction. He accepted the offer and retreated to Worcester, Massachusetts, two days ride west of Boston, to become a schoolmaster.

At first, he was a terrible schoolmaster. He was so bad that he began to sympathize with Master Cleverly. John lacked Master Marsh's talent for seeing future leaders in his students. He wrote in his diary, "They are only a large number of little runtlings, just capable of lisping 'A-B-C' and troubling me."

Living so far from home made John feel lonely. He began to keep a diary as a way of talking to himself: "Everything seems so dry and lifeless after the exciting times at Harvard. Here in Worcester I have no intricate discussions, no hot debates, no daily news of Europe fresh from the docks of Boston. Where is the fellowship and fun? Hope," he sighed, "has left me."

All his self-doubts tumbled together and seemed to accuse him. In his diary he criticized himself viciously. "I'm changeable and vain. I'm full of foolishness and false pride. I must begin to organize my life, to read the books that will teach me to become a better . . . a better *what?* What will I be? A doctor? A farmer? A scientist? Surely, something more than a schoolmaster!"

But his natural curiosity overcame his frustration. In a few months the boys and girls in his classroom began to fascinate him. "My schoolroom is made up of kings, clowns, politicians, bishops, fops, fools, fiddlers, flatterers, dandies, chimney sweepers, and every other character drawn in history or seen in the world!"

He had fun seeing himself as the emperor of a complicated society that carried out his imperial orders. "I have several renowned generals that are only three feet high. I have several deep-scheming politicians in petticoats. I have others catching and dissecting flies, accumulating remarkable pebbles, cockleshells, &c, with as much curiosity as any genius in the Royal Society."

John never made fun of them or their collections or their games. He found that praise worked better than sarcasm and punishment. "Commendation enlivens and stimulates them," he wrote to himself. He praised them, but not too much. He wanted a word of praise to be valuable and not "cheap." Being a schoolmaster did not excite him, but it became restful. He knew that education was important and, as long as he was teaching, he meant to "drive from these tender minds everything that is mean or little."

He was not as energetic as Master Marsh and often acted too much like his imaginary emperor. He assigned older boys to read tiresome lessons and conduct the class while he sat at his desk translating Latin poems or reading new books.

In some ways, his easy years as Worcester's schoolmaster were important. Isolated, far from Boston politics and controversy, he began to hunger for debate, for testing his ideas against other ideas. This lull after the intense years at Harvard made him realize that his life's work—whatever it was—would somehow use his argumentative Yankee nature to hammer out ideas, as the blacksmith hammered out red-hot iron. He knew that his words could strike hot sparks from worthy colleagues and opponents. His impatience and ambition rose like the tide in the marsh. John Adams was hungry to do great things.

Polite Worcester society loved this charming young man from Braintree, so bright and amusing, full of praise for their fine houses and pretty daughters. He was a good dancer and could pick out a tune on the dulcimer or flute. He debated Worcester intellectuals on political and church issues, displaying his brilliant mind and his bull terrier's energy.

He could often be found at the home of Dr. Nahum Willard, reading his medical books. Mrs. Willard tried unsuccessfully to discourage him from chewing tobacco. Many Worcester friends discouraged him from reading the medical books at all: The imaginative young man began to imagine that he had many of the diseases he read about. "Am I flushed?" he would ask friends. "Yes, I'm flushed. I think a have a fever. Are there dark spots on my tongue? Ahhhhhhh!" He would display his perfectly normal tongue to them. "I may very well be dying of Sperry's Disease. Or palm frond jaundice. Perhaps I should purge myself with some jalap or *cremor tartar*. Perhaps I should strengthen my blood with Daffy's Elixir!"

John had many remarkable talents. He was small and round but quite handsome, charming, polite, witty, and honest. True, all his friends had to admit that he was the stubbornest and most argumentative Yankee they had ever met; this tenacity could, however, be of great value in one profession: the law.

John became friends with James Putnam, a Worcester lawyer. He talked about the law with Putnam for months, attending court cases and watching Putnam. For John, the law was an interpretation of Puritan beliefs. Law insisted on good order in society. It upheld harmony and equality of thought. It was a code of right and justice, and a direct interpretation of scriptural morals. He could see that imperfect men made laws to improve an imperfect world. John Adams wanted to be a part of improving the world and the lives of everyone in it.

But for John there was another side to the law just as appealing as ideas and morals. For John, the practice of law was a little like the theater. A trial was an important play with real consequences. It had drama in the dispute between parties, in crimes against the colony, and in the way a lawyer might use his words and manner to win the jury's trust. With his love for oratory, debate, reading aloud, singing, and making himself noticed, John Adams was a secret actor, a ham.

He had, at last, found his profession: He would become a lawyer.

In 1756, at the age of twenty-one, he apprenticed himself to James Putnam. Apprenticeship was a very old way of learning a trade. A young man lived and worked with a master of a trade. The apprentice gave his labor and usually paid a fee (Putnam requested a hundred pounds "when it was convenient to pay") for working lessons in carpentry, blacksmithing, soapmaking, or any trade that required intricate knowledge.

John moved in with James Putnam and his wife for two years. He continued to teach school but studied law books every night. He did legal research for Putnam and learned to write some of the simple documents—deeds, letters to the court, wills—as Putnam's helper.

It was a long, tiring schedule and Putnam wasn't always a good teacher. He may have been jealous of John's intelligence, or he may have mistaken John's optimistic honesty for arrogance. This was an easy mistake to make. John could be sweet and smart but he could also be the most annoying man in Massachusetts.

John taught through the day, argued about law,

politics, and philosophy with Putnam at dinner, and studied at night. John was almost always exhausted. In his weariness, all the imagined illnesses he'd learned began to appear. His friend Dr. Willard may have realized his sickness wasn't real, so he prescribed a soothing diet of milk, bread, vegetables, and no meat. John wrote to a college friend, "I'm terribly sick. The diet Dr. Willard has given me may have saved my life but it also gives me heartburn unless I drink pots of strong tea."

In 1757, there was a war going on at the frontiers of the colonies. The British ruled the colonies of the seacoast—from Massachusetts (which then included Maine) in the north to Georgia in the south. The French held the great Mississippi River Valley and large parts of what would become Canada. Britain and France had been in and out of war with one another for more than a hundred years, but in this dispute over colonial expansion and borders the French enlisted the aid of the fierce, merciless Iroquois tribes: It was called the French and Indian War.

Four thousand British soldiers under Lord Jeffrey Amherst passed through Worcester on their way to Lake George. John Adams found them a delightful distraction. He wrote about them in his diary: "The officers were very social. They spent their evenings and took their suppers with some of the Worcester families. They entertained us with their music and their dances. Many of them were Scotsmen in their plaids. Their music was delightful, and even the bagpipe was not disagreeable."

John believed in order and tradition. He was proud to see the disciplined ranks of British soldiers defending them against the savage Iroquois. "I rejoiced that I was an Englishman, and gloried in the name of Britain."

Between 1756 and 1758, John Adams learned some law from books. Putnam was a lazy fellow in his own work, though, and didn't teach John a great deal about practical law. John was well liked in Worcester, so when his two-year apprenticeship was over, some wanted him to stay in town as a lawyer and as the Register of Deeds. But John couldn't find two essential things in Worcester: He needed to compete with the very best, and the best lawyers in the colony were in Boston; he also needed "the sea breeze and the pure zephyrs from the rocky mountains of my native town." He returned to live with his parents in the marshes of Braintree.

A new lawyer must be admitted to the association of local lawyers—their "bar." James Putnam, out of jealousy or simple laziness, didn't write letters of recommendation to the Boston Bar for Adams. Unfazed and characteristically cocky, John set out for Boston to approach its four most famous lawyers.

Old Jeremiah Gridley, patriarch of the Bar, was impressed by Adams. He offered to lend him his precious law books, suggested a course of study, and treated him like a grandfather. "I have a few pieces of advice to give you, Mr. Adams. One is to pursue the study of the law, not the gain you may make from it. Pursue the gain enough to keep out of the briar bushes, but give your main attention to the study of it. The next is not to marry early, for an early marriage will obstruct your improvement and cause you expense."

Oxenbridge Thacher had studied with Gridley. Both Gridley and Thacher, like Adams, had entered Harvard to prepare for the ministry, but turned to the law. He was a plain, welcoming man who was kind to John. He agreed with Gridley's plan of study, and promised his help.

Benjamin Pratt had also studied with Gridley. He was gruff and cold. John didn't know, when they met, that Pratt was in almost constant pain—his leg had been awkwardly amputated when he was a boy. Though John didn't like him at first, he came to admire and respect him.

The fourth lawyer John met that week proved to be one of the great men of his life. James Otis was a fiery figure in the Massachusetts courts, a man of enormous intellect, ego, and passion. John was awestruck by the wild and brilliant Otis, and by the way his courtroom voice shook jury and judge alike. Otis liked John Adams immediately. He promised the boy his help at the bar.

As much as he loved his Braintree marshes,

John was fascinated by Boston's frantic life, like an anthill of humanity. In November 1759, John Adams rode up to Boston with his friend Sam Quincy, who had apprenticed with Benjamin Pratt. They were presented to the judge of the Superior Court, recommended by Gridley, and sworn in as officers of the Massachusetts court.

Within a few weeks John Adams had his first case as a lawyer in Braintree, *Lambert v. Field*. John represented Field. He lost.

It was a local matter. Two of Luke Lambert's horses broke into Joseph Field's garden and trampled his crops. Field discovered the horses at about the same time that Lambert came for them. Field yelled at Lambert to stop, but Lambert waved his hat and whooped, shooing his horses out of the garden, and then left without discussing the damages. It was an open and shut case in Field's favor.

Lazy James Putnam had never shown John Adams how to prepare precise legal forms, called "writs." But Lambert's lawyer was Sam Quincy, who had received three years of careful teaching with Benjamin Pratt. The justice hearing the case was Josiah Quincy, Sam's father. John's writ failed to identify the county in which the damages were caused, and didn't mention the constables of Braintree as the authorities in that county. Josiah Quincy threw the case out of court on this technicality. Defeated by a lout like Lambert and his best friend, John looked like a fool in Braintree. Learning to be a lawyer and a man of his father's wise reputation would be a long, uphill road.

The Parlor

"Guns, girls, cards, flutes, and violins stand between me and my books," John sighed. He and Richard Cranch were coming back from a hike with their dogs in the Blue Hills. "I'm so lazy! I get up late and don't even make a fire. By ten o'clock my fire might be crackling but I still don't have the gumption to open my law books. No, I'm too easily distracted by anything—a pipe, thinking about a girl, writing a poem, the latest issue of *The Spectator*, reading a play, writing a love letter. . . ."

"A love letter, John! Are you serious about keeping company with Hannah Quincy?" Richard asked.

"Am I keeping company with her, or am I part of her company of suitors?"

"Sure, she's a pretty thing."

"Yessuh. Pretty as a porcelain doll."

"And wealthy."

"Hmm." John reached down to scratch Ruby's long ears. "I s'pect her dowry would be considerable."

"So?"

"Well, Richard, I'm thinkin' on it. I need a wife. A wife would give me ballast and I'd have more direction. But Hannah is a flirt. Is she serious or does she just want to collect more men than any other woman on Massachusetts Bay?"

"Only one way to tell: Ask her to marry you."

"Well, that's like the fellah that wanted to fly, Richard. There was only one way to tell if he could or not. So he went up on the roof . . . and gave up the idea of flying."

They laughed, and the dogs raced on ahead of them toward the ocean.

In 1759, John Adams's lazy days were more active

than many men's active days. Though he was distracted by girls and hunting, parties and silly magazines, he was also studying serious law books and getting clients. He was learning to write bulletproof writs and arguing cases in Braintree, Germantown, Weymouth, Abington, and even Boston. He spent a lot of time in the saddle, trotting from court to court.

There was a lively set of young men and women within trotting distance. There were parties with games and plays and dinners. He was often in Braintree, competing for Hannah Quincy's attention. Late one evening they sat in her parents' parlor alone, an uncomfortable silence between them, the kind of ominous quiet that settles in before some special event.

Hannah hurried the hoped-for event along. "Mr. Adams," she said prettily, "I do think you are entirely too serious about your studies of the law and of those old Romans."

"Truly, Miss Quincy? They haven't ever distracted me from you, have they?"

"Perhaps not, sir. But I speak of a general attitude. Just suppose you were in your study with your law

books and Latins, and your wife—supposing you had one—walked in to break your concentration? Would you be angry with her?"

"Why, a man would be a villain and a beast to show anger to his wife if she broke in accidentally. And no wife of mine would willingly disturb her hard-working husband at his labors."

"What kind of wife would your wife be, Mr. Adams?" Hannah asked, fluttering her very sweet eyes.

"Why, Miss Quincy, I suppose she would be very much like you." He was suddenly aware of her perfume, the darkness of her eyes, and the delicacy of her hands as they adjusted her shawl. "In truth, Miss Quincy, now that we're speaking of husbands and wives . . ."

"Yes, Mr. Adams?" Her voice was low and caressing.

"John Adams!"

Jonathan Sewall's voice not only startled John into leaping up from the couch, but somehow conjured up the face of old Jeremiah Gridley growling, "Do not marry early, young man, for an early marriage will obstruct your improvement!"

"Adams!" Sewall went on. "True, I haven't seen ye for an age—a week at least—but I'm not a ghost, John. You look all pale and trembling. Has Miss Quincy been telling you ghost stories?"

"I believe Mr. Adams has frightened himself," Hannah said with a satisfied smile.

"Then tell us the ghost story, John," Jonathan said. "But first, introductions. You know Esther Quincy, of course. But allow me to introduce you to Mr. Bela Lincoln?"

Hannah Quincy's eyes flashed on Lincoln like a cat peering at a mouse. "Mr. Lincoln, you look splendid in your uniform. Those boots are so dashing and that sword looks positively lethal. Have you come to conquer us all, Lieutenant Lincoln?"

"*Captain* Lincoln," Bela replied with some pride, "and such a capture would be of the greatest interest to me."

Color returned to John Adams's cheeks and he breathed a sigh of relief. A dangerous moment had passed and another mouse had taken his place.

A few weeks later, Hannah and Captain Lincoln

of the Germantown Militia announced their engagement.

Was John relieved or upset? Had he let the most wonderful woman in his life slip away because of his law books? Had he been too timid? "Richard," he said to his friend a few days later, "let's take our rifles and walk in the hills to soothe my brain. I don't know whether I've just avoided a disaster or missed a great opportunity for happiness."

The Visitors' Gallery

It was fortunate that John was early for the trial, because there was a crowd behind him, pushing and jostling to enter the courtroom. But he had known it would be a popular spectacle. Boston was a town of merchants and politicians, and the issue being discussed was important to everyone.

The merchants of Boston had challenged a British law. Representing the Boston merchants were the precise and brilliant Oxenbridge Thacher and the fiery James Otis. The case for the Crown—for the colony of Massachusetts, in this case—was given to John's friend and Boston's legal patriarch, Jeremiah Gridley.

142

What a battle!

The British Parliament took sour notice of what it was spending on the French and Indian War and defending and expanding its American colonies. Parliament looked for a way to get some of the money back. One promising solution was to strictly enforce the taxes on imported goods. But import taxes were so high, and the enforcement so loose, that smuggling or buying them from non-British suppliers was common.

To collect taxes, Crown customs officials asked for "writs of assistance." These were broad search warrants, documents allowing them to break into any ship, home, warehouse, or business to search for untaxed goods. Boston merchants had asked the chief judge of the colony's highest court to examine the legality of these search warrants.

John sat in the visitors' gallery and looked at the court crowd with a professional eye. There were a great many important people here. There was his cousin, Sam Adams, who was becoming a political figure with a reputation as a troublemaker. There was John's friend, the wealthy merchant (and smuggler) John Hancock. Even Benjamin Pratt had made his painful way to the court.

It started quietly enough. Gridley laid out the Crown's case, citing the legality of the writs and the basis for them in English law and Parliamentary decrees. Ox Thacher came back with a string of dull precedents—court decisions against the writs. Thacher's argument had nothing to do with the right or wrong of the writs but argued that they should be issued by a special admiralty court with authority over ships and oceans. John was bored.

Then James Otis rose to speak. John saw that Thacher's meek, bookish opening had been a trick, a whispered introduction so that Otis's peals of thunder would sound even louder. "This writ," Otis boomed, "is against the fundamental principles of law!"

John Adams's head snapped up from his notes. Otis was not referring to law books and technicalities, but to the very ideas of right and wrong.

"It appears to me the worst instrument of arbitrary power, the most destructive of English liberty and the fundamental principles of law, that ever was found in an English law-book. . . .

"Every one with this writ may be a tyrant. . . . A person with this writ, in the daytime, may enter all houses, shops, &c, at will, and command all to assist him. . . . One of the most essential branches of English liberty is the freedom of one's house. A man's house is his castle . . . but this writ, if it should be declared legal, would totally annihilate this privilege. Custom-house officers may . . . enter, may break locks, bars, and everything in their way; and whether they break through malice or revenge, no man, no court, can inquire.

"What a scene does this open! Every man, prompted by revenge, ill-humor, or wantonness, to inspect the inside of his neighbor's house, may get a writ of assistance. Others will ask it from self-defense; one writ will provoke another, until society be involved in tumult and in blood."

Even the judges in their scarlet robes, huge judicial wigs, and broad black hats were caught up in Otis's passion. Yes, this was the eloquence John had come to hear, but he ignored the beauty of the words and heard instead the drumbeat of the unquestionable meaning. John kept writing it down:

"Every man [is naturally] an independent sovereign, subject to no law but the law written on his heart and revealed to him by his Maker. . . .

"No person or thing could rightfully contest his right to his life, his liberty. Nor was his right to his property less incontestable. The club that he had snapped from a tree, for a staff or for defense, was his own. His bow and arrow were his own; if by a pebble he had killed a partridge or a squirrel, it was his own. No creature, man or beast, had a right to take it from him."

James Otis's blast against writs of assistance awoke something large and frightening in John Adams. That moment changed him forever.

"These rights are inherent and inalienable. . . . The security of these rights to life, liberty, and property have been the object of all the struggles against arbitrary power, temporal and spiritual, civil and political, military and ecclesiastical—in every age."

There in the visitors' gallery, John had a painfully clear vision. The contrast between Britain and America snapped into focus. He saw that America was a new place with its own new and hopeful values. He saw that Britain was stuck in the mire of old European ideas about kings and noble families. In Britain, the rights of "common" men could not stand against "noble" kings and lords. Common homes were legally ransacked. Common men were legally impressed—kidnapped into the Royal Navy without their consent. America was a new place with unlimited potential. In this fresh land, every man was noble. God had made it so. No king, no unnatural or invalid law could change it.

Otis went on and on. He and Thacher impressed the judges and the spectators but it was an unsuccessful effort. The right of the Crown to search without cause was declared valid. Their argument against injustice, however, opened a dangerous crack between the mother country of Britain and the colonies of America that would not close.

Years and years later, Adams would remember that moment to a friend, and say, "Then and there the child Independence was born."

In few months, another moral earthquake shook John Adams.

The influenza epidemic of 1761 struck especially angrily at older citizens of Braintree. Seventeen of the village elders died. Deacon Adams was one of them.

"He was the honestest man I ever knew," John said to Richard Cranch. What he could not say, because his heart was too full of grief, was that Deacon Adams was his ideal of goodness and kindness and strength. John Adams's entire life was modeled on that of his father—a man who had never been more than a few dozen miles from the Adams marsh.

Susanna Adams survived the epidemic but was too sick to attend the simple Puritan service in the graveyard next to the common. After the burial, John took his dogs and his rifle and walked deep into the Blue Hills. It would be many weeks before light would return to his heart. His had lost his best friend.

But he was about to gain another.

The Bridge

"Some invest their money in mills, some in live-stock," the deacon had told John, "but I never knew a piece of land to break or run away." Much of what Deacon Adams earned from making shoes and harnesses had gone to the church and the poor of Braintree. Piece by piece, however, he bought land.

Upon his death, Peter inherited the Adams house, where Susanna lived, and the original farm. Elihu took possession of a fine farm in the village of Randolph, to the south. It had been agreed that the smallest share would go to John, because his Harvard education had been expensive. But this smallest share was a joy. John was now the owner of the farm next to the deacon's original acres. His own saltbox house now stood a few yards away from the house in which he was born.

John was now a freeholder—he owned the land on which he lived. He had a vote in the town elections, and could hold public office. More important, he had an *obligation* to hold office. In his first year as a freeholder, John was appointed surveyor of roads for the town of Braintree.

He didn't want the job. He knew nothing about building roads. John Quincy took him aside and said, "Young Adams, ability and privilege carry responsibility. Yessuh. Y'fathah was a selectman f'years. Didn't want to do it—lots of work, carin' f'the less fortunate, seein' to widows, orphans, n'such. Did it, though. Good job of it too. You'll do fine."

That summer, John Adams was involved in building a new stone bridge across Town Brook. The bridge seized his imagination. To him, the simple stone arch was a symbol: a bridge between the narrow paths of his youth and his way in the larger world. He checked on its progress every day. He watched the workmen prepare the buttresses, the twin foundations on either side of the arch that would bear the load of the bridge. John saw the necessity of their mutual strength, how they supported one another. The bridge's geometry was useless without that twin footing. There was a lesson there he couldn't quite grasp.

His legal work kept him in the saddle much of the time. His business took him more and more to Weymouth, especially since his friend Richard Cranch had become engaged to Parson Smith's daughter, Mary. John began to spend evenings with Richard and Mary. A fly in the Weymouth soup was Mary's younger sister, Abigail.

Abigail Smith annoyed John Adams. She was much too bold and had too many opinions. Some of them actually contradicted his. She talked too much. Almost as much as he talked. She had a pigeon-toed walk and sat on the couch, or even the floor, with her legs crossed under her skirts, very unladylike. She did not giggle and sniffle like a proper young lady but had a boyish, open laugh.

Only a child of seventeen, she was educated beyond her place in life. Abby read entirely too much, and not merely novels about manners and romance. No, she read philosophy and history, as if she were a man!

Worst of all, she had an insufferably calm look, as if she understood all the complex political and philosophical thoughts John declared with dramatic flourish. He found it disrespectful and insulting, the way she actually looked amused when he dropped a pickled herring on his waistcoat. And she laughed aloud when he caught his heel on the hearth corner and fell onto the dog. She would not be appropriately meek in a conversation. Her older sister would sip her tea properly and nod sweetly when men's matters were being discussed—like the furor over the writs of assistance. Not Abigail. She had actually argued with one of the Weymouth selectmen about the writs. True, John also disagreed with the nasty old stick-in-the-mud, but it wasn't proper for young ladies to dispute with gentlemen. She was troublesome, presumptuous, arrogant, disrespectful, and unladylike.

It was five miles from Parson Smith's in Weymouth, across Penn's Hill, to John's house on the Braintree marsh. Sometimes he fumed and spluttered all the way home in the dark over some ridiculous thing Abby Smith had said. The conceit of the girl!

One night he stopped on his new stone bridge and leaned back on his mare's quarters with one hand, looking at the buttress on one side and then at the other. The two stubborn pillars of impervious stone supported one another and held up the almost magical geometry of the load-bearing arch.

A strange and surprising thought crept over him. He and Abigail were like two strong buttresses that supported one another and held up a traffic of thought, wit, and love.

John and Abigail didn't just fall in love. They simply recognized that they belonged to one another—heart, soul, mind, and body. In a way no one could explain, they ceased to become two people. They thought with one mind, doubly broad with a doubly powerful will. They often disagreed, and often argued passionately, but always with unquestioned love, until they determined the truth of a thing together. Abby was the natural and assured counterpart to John's awkward self-doubt. From that time on, every moment they spent apart was painful.

Once they knew they belonged to one another, they were in no hurry to rush life. Mrs. Smith thought her daughter could find a better suitor with a more important family. Parson Smith wondered about John Adams's changing political views—were they too radical? But John and Abby had no doubts. It would happen.

John's law practice required him to ride everywhere and see hundreds of people. He would certainly meet people with contagious diseases, and the recurring smallpox epidemics had been especially deadly in the 1760s. John decided, for Abby's sake, to be inoculated against the disease. At the time, this meant being purposely infected with a mild case of smallpox. It was dangerous but, when it worked, effective. Almost as bad as the smallpox was the wrong-headed medical "preparation" for the inoculation: being dosed with strong laxatives and emetics (to induce vomiting). John and his brother Peter went together to be quarantined for weeks in a Boston hospital. Abigail and John began to write to one another, often more than once a day.

Later, when John was riding his long court circuit, arguing cases to the south in Martha's Vineyard or north in what would become Maine, they wrote more letters to one another. Over many years, events that shook the world kept them apart for long periods, but their letters continued. They were sometimes passionate love letters, sometimes practical notes and reminders, but they always carried their keen thoughts on the extraordinary events that surrounded them. These thousands of letters made up the most intelligent, important, and historical correspondence of an age.

On October 25, 1764, Parson Smith performed the ceremony that married John Adams, free-holder of Braintree, to his daughter, Abigail Smith Adams. They would need their double strength for the times to come.

The Docks

Jeremiah Gridley had died, and the magnificent intellect of James Otis was sputtering away into madness. By 1767, John Adams had become the most sought-after and active lawyer in Boston. His list of cases and clients was long and distinguished. He put in long hours at court and in the saddle. But he was a Swamp Yankee farmer in his heart. He needed the smell of earth. For a terrier like John, the only rest from work of the mind was work of the body.

In Braintree he was a blur of activity. Visiting friends found him in the fields with his hired help, laughing and shouting as they cleared brush and dug drainage ditches. He was building stone fences, pruning the fruit trees, spreading manure, digging stumps, prying up stones, and building stone fences (most of the fences didn't keep anything in or out; they were just a way to get the stones out of the fields). Come spring, they found the boxy little lawyer plowing behind six oxen or seeding or weeding.

Abigail was just as busy, just as happy. Their first child, Nabby, was nearly two. Abigail was pregnant with their second child but carried on, doing her own spinning, weaving, sewing, baking, cooking, and butter churning. She and John had help from Judah, one of the foundling girls Deacon Adams had rescued years before (the cause of another loud argument between Susanna and the deacon). Susanna, herself, lived next door, as peppery as ever but much happier now that she had found a loving friend in Abigail.

If the American colonies were doing as well as the Adams family, the prospects for Massachusetts would be sunny and pleasant. But the outlook for the colonies was bleak. Resentment and anger against Britain had reached a dangerous level.

In 1760, the British Empire had crowned a new king, George III. He was only a few years older than John Adams, and almost as stubborn. He schemed to take back much of the power his grandfather, George II, had lost to Parliament. Part of his plan was to "make the American colonies pay for the expense of saving them," in the French and Indian War. The Peace of Paris in 1763 had made Britain the strongest European and colonial power. Britain's navy controlled the world's oceans. The American colonies had been enormously enlarged to include Canada and the Mississippi River Valley. But the war had been expensive.

In 1764, Parliament saddled the colonies with the Sugar Act. Taxes on sugar and molasses were lowered but enforcement increased. Taxes were raised on British goods—cloth, coffee, indigo (for dyeing cloth), and wines from the Canary Islands. Non-British rum and French wines were made illegal. The tax, itself, was bad enough, but the ruthless enforcement of the Act by the Royal

Navy—boarding American ships, impressing sailors, ransacking cargoes—was infuriating.

In 1765, tax revenues from the colonies were still unsatisfactory, so Parliament enacted the Stamp Act. This was a straightforward money-making scheme: wills, contracts, court decisions, and licenses were not legal unless they were written on paper with an expensive government stamp. Once again, the tax was merely tiresome but the method was insulting. During the Parliamentary debate on the Stamp Act, the colonies sent representatives to offer the American view. Parliament saw no reason to hear them, assuring them that the colonies had no influence on the laws that governed them.

When word of this snub came back to Boston, an angry cry was heard on the docks: "Taxation without representation!" There were violent riots, some of them encouraged by a growing band of anti-British toughs, the Liberty Boys, also known as the Sons of Liberty. John Adams didn't care for the dock-front ruffians that made up most of that rowdy band in Boston, though his cousin Sam Adams was one of their leaders. John preferred to fight Britain's unjust laws with logic and rhetoric. He wrote a series of powerful articles in the Boston *Gazette* which were later reprinted in London as *The True Sentiments of America*. It wasn't a call for armed revolt, but a carefully built argument for just treatment of Britain's citizens in the Colonies.

But Massachusetts was angry. Even in the more genteel parlors of Beacon Hill and Cambridge there was protest—insulted Massachusetts families refused to buy British goods or drink British tea. Homespun clothing became fashionable. Riots and protests broke out in almost every colony, right down the coast to the Carolinas. Many stamp tax collectors were tarred and feathered by angry Americans.

The Stamp Act caused so much trouble that it was repealed in a year. The more widespread Townshend Acts followed it. Parliament knew that in 1767 the colonies were just beginning to build up their industries. Britain's factories were already humming. The new act fixed high taxes on manufactured products the colonies needed: glass, lead, paint, paper, and tea.

One basic problem was that the colonies had no direct connection to the British Parliament. They tried to appeal to Britain through their colonial governors. When Massachusetts towns sent their views on the debate over taxes and representation to the legislature, John Adams wrote "Instructions of the town of Braintree" to their assembly delegates. Its words flew like sparks to the other towns and to other colonies: "We have always understood it to be a grand and fundamental principle of English law that no freeman should be subject to any tax to which he has not given his own consent."

But Parliament would not relent. The new taxes and the new insult to American colonists sparked real rebellion. Smuggling goods past British taxes became a popular (and profitable) act of defiance in Massachusetts. The Royal Navy frigate *Romney* was dispatched to Boston with Royal Marines to protect its tax collectors.

In 1768, John Hancock needed the best lawyer in Boston. He summoned his old friend John Adams. Wealthy Hancock owned a fleet of merchant ships. His sloop *Liberty* had been seized by

the customs officials. A tax collector had impru-
dently pushed his way aboard the *Liberty* when it
docked, and someone had locked him in the captain's cabin. While the tax collector was banging at
the door, several barrels of untaxed Madeira wine
were unloaded. In punishment, the Crown seized
the *Liberty* and its cargo, and levied a fine on the
sloop's captain.

In court, John Adams was persuasive in arguing
that a mild and beneficial law could be interpreted
loosely, but a severe law—like the Townshend
Acts—must be interpreted strictly. In this strict
interpretation, could it be proven decisively that
John Hancock, the ship's owner, knew anything
about a few barrels of wine unloaded in the dark?
Was it strictly established that even the captain
knew about the wine or about its unloading?
Perhaps the ship's owner or the captain would
have paid duty for the wine but it was stolen by a
few "frolicsome" sailors.

Adams asked the court if the punishment truly
fit this crime. Perhaps a lesser amount of duty was
lost to the Crown. Was it fair to fine the captain,

who was not incontrovertibly guilty? Should the owner forfeit both the cargo and the sloop?

Finally, he suggested that Boston men were being punished under "a law made without our consent." Was any of this fair?

The judge would not publicly agree with John Adams, but delayed and dragged the case out until Crown prosecutors withdrew the charges.

A year later, a more serious and disturbing case came to John Adams.

The Massachusetts brig *Pitt Packett* was homeward bound and in Massachusetts waters when it was overhauled by the Royal Navy sloop *Rose*. The British lieutenant needed a few extra sailors and meant to impress them from the *Pitt*. Four of the *Pitt* sailors had been in the Royal Navy and knew the inhuman conditions they would endure aboard *Rose*. They barricaded themselves in the hold and refused to be brought out. They defended themselves with one musket, a fish spear, and a harpoon. More Royal Marines arrived from the *Rose* and they rushed the hold. The musket went off harmlessly, but in the dark hold, the harpoon sliced into the neck of the lieutenant. He died in minutes.

All four men were arrested for "piracy and murder on the high seas." Hanging seemed inevitable.

Fifteen Crown judges were assembled for the trial. Adams requested a trial by a jury of the sailors' peers, Massachusetts men, but was denied. John's close friend Jonathan Sewall was the prosecutor and laid out the facts of the sailors' defiance of authority, their stubborn barricade, the death of a Royal Navy officer. It seemed like an open and shut case.

Not to John Adams. He had before him a copy of the British *Statutes of Laws*, which forbade impressment of sailors in American waters. The book was large and John had it laid out on the defense table in front of the judges. He rose and addressed the court: "May it please Your Excellencies and Your Honors, my defense of the prisoners is that the melancholy action for which they stand accused is justifiable homicide, and therefore no crime at all."

John started to outline his defense, but to everyone's surprise, Crown Governor Bernard lurched to his feet and moved that the judges adjourn to council chambers. The jury included the Admiralty Judge in charge of maritime matters, and Commodore Hood, ranking officer of the Royal Navy on the American coast. Adams's hope was dashed. His carefully crafted arguments based on English Common Law and Admiralty Law were unheard. He sat down with a thump.

He went home to Abigail and talked half the night. How could he help these desperate sailors?

Next morning, the fifteen judges sat without expression. The courtroom was silent. Governor Bernard rose to his feet, wiped a bit of sweat from his brow, then spoke: "It is . . ." He cleared his throat, a long silence. "It is the judgement of this court that the defendants in the matter of the *Pitt* are not guilty. The killing of Lt. Panton was justifiable homicide in necessary self-defense."

Before even a shout of triumph could escape the crowd, the Admiralty Judge leaped to his feet and screeched, "The judgement of the court is unanimous!" and the judges filed out as if the courtroom were on fire. The colony's Chief Justice Hutchinson, an old friend of John's, had seen the *Statutes of Laws* on John's table, determined John's line of argument, and decided that any word about impressment might cause a public riot. John's finest chance for oratory had passed with only a few words.

In the saddle again, John rode the weary circuit of the Massachusetts court—north as far as Falmouth (in what is now Maine), over to Worcester, down to Plymouth. He was a hero to Sam Adams and the Liberty Boys, a trusted legal counselor to one of the wealthiest men in Boston, John Hancock, and a respected voice in all of Massachusetts.

Naturally talkative and gregarious, had also had a habit of listening in silence. He would find a tavern for his night's lodgings, see to his little mare, and sit at a dark corner table, absorbing the talk and the feelings of the people. Freedom from British tyranny was the most common thread.

"Liberty Tree" poles erected by the Sons of Liberty were erected on many village commons. Fewer and fewer taverns were named "The King George."

He missed his family and they missed him. Abigail wrote to him, "Sunday seems a more lonesome day to me than any other when you are absent." His daughter Nabby rocked her little brother, John Quincy, with her own lullaby:

Come, Papa, come home,
Home to Brother Johnny.

His mare's gait and the seat of the saddle were a good place for him to think, even in the snow. Sam Adams, John Hancock, and others wanted him to be a stirring voice in the argument for liberty. Philosophically, he stood with them. But he was a stubbornly traditional man. A part of him believed that Britain would see the sense of embracing the colonies with a more motherly warmth. The rest of him detected no hope for a compromise. Would he join their speeches?

He neither liked nor trusted the rabble of Boston—the dregs of the docks, idle toughs. He wanted to persuade minds and hearts, not to spark bonfires in dry tinder. As for liberty, he wanted it for himself: He wanted the kind of independence of thought he had admired in his father and in Colonel John Quincy. No, he would keep a little distance for now, and think.

John Adams rode on through the snow, doing the work of justice.

The Street

The winter of 1769 and 1770 was grim. In February, John and Abigail's daughter Susanna died. She was not quite a year old. John Adams sank into grief and could not speak about his lost child for years.

An inevitable clash of passions called him out of his grief.

Boston was seething with anger. Royal soldiers were quartered in the city to "keep the peace," but almost daily scuffles and brawls flared up between them and Boston's ruffians. The town was garrisoned with these "British lobsterbacks" wearing bright red coats with white cross-belts, polished brass buttons and buckles, and tall black hats. They stood out like a handful of cranberries in a bowl of Boston beans. The town was also swarming with idle apprentices, out-of-work smugglers, hard-drinking sailors, and the usual dock loafers— all of them spoiling for a fight.

A boy had been accidentally killed when a mob surrounded the house of a British sympathizer. The street gang threw bricks and beat at the Brit's door with clubs. When they broke into his house, he fired his musket blindly, killing a young apprentice. The sympathizer was seized and carried away. He barely escaped hanging.

The apprentice's funeral was mounted by the Sons of Liberty as a propaganda event. Five hundred children marched solemnly at the head, followed by six of the boy's friends carrying the coffin. The town turned out, as the coffin made its way from the Liberty Tree on the commons, to the town house, and up to the burying ground. John Adams made a note in his diary: "My eyes never beheld such a funeral; the procession extended further than can be well imagined. This shows there are many more lives to spend, if wanted, in the service of their country."

Boston was a powder keg looking for a match.

Monday, March 5, 1770, was a knife-edge day. Several fist fights and shouting matches had broken out in the snow. That evening, a detachment of soldiers had been accosted by a mob of toughs with clubs. Surrounded, they raised their muskets and were about to blast a way to safety when an officer rushed up and marched them into a nearby yard. The angry crowd moved on toward the town house square.

Outside the hated customs house, trying to keep warm, stood a lone sentry in the pale light of a crescent moon. The ugly crowd rumbled into the square and immediately surrounded him, shouting "Kill him! Knock the bloody brute down!"

The sentry retreated up the stairs and cocked his musket.

"If anyone touches me, I'll fire!" the sentry called, and then yelled at the top of his voice, "Sergeant of the Guard! Post number one!"

The barracks were only half a block away, and

the soldiers were expecting some alarm. A sergeant with seven men rushed out of the barracks in full kit. They jogged in step, their equipment jangling in rhythm, through the startled crowd to form a rank in front of the threatened sentry. There were catcalls, insults, shouts.

Captain Thomas Preston, the officer on watch, sprinted out of the barracks clutching his sword and joined his men. In addition to the sentry, there were now nine British soldiers, with single-shot muskets, facing several dozen furious men armed with clubs, sticks, and bricks. Close to the muskets stood a massive African-American freeman, Crispus Attucks, taunting the lobsterbacks and daring them to fire. The situation was precisely what the Sons of Liberty wanted to set off the powder keg.

The mob began to throw snowballs, then pieces of ice, stones, sharp oyster shells, and bricks. "You are cowardly rascals," came a cry. Then, "Fire! Fire! Why don't you fire?" A tough from the crowd grabbed a musket by its bayonet and tried to tear it out of the marine's hands.

A shot! Then a ragged volley of six more shots! The crowd ran for the shadows, leaving three dead men in the snow. Crispus Attucks, at the front, was the first to die.

The soldiers were more frightened than the crowd. Preston hurried them into a column and marched them off to the barracks at double-time. The crowd returned and claimed their dead.

Within fifteen minutes church bells were ringing and all of Boston was stumbling into the dark streets. The mob grew to a great crowd. Rumors flew—hundreds dead, great massacre of innocents, a marine regiment charged a peaceful crowd of friends. The noise of the mob grew.

The calmest and most commanding man on the scene was Governor Hutchinson, who had been one of the judges in Adams's trial defending the four *Pitt* sailors. Hutchinson appeared on the balcony of the town house and waited for the crowd to settle into quiet. "A terrible crisis has seized our city!" he shouted to the crowd. "Three of our citizens are dead. More violence will only darken the catastrophe. Our best resource at this moment is the law! I promise you that I will immediately form a court of inquiry into the matter. If the soldiers involved are found guilty, they will be punished by the law, in whatever fashion the law directs! The law shall have its course," he shouted at last. "I will live and die by the law."

All the British soldiers in the city were marched to barracks, leaving only a guard around the court of inquiry. Captain Preston and all nine soldiers were arrested by city authorities and charged with murder.

Captain Preston knew that his men were as good as hanged if he didn't find skillful legal counsel. Even lawyers sympathetic to British interests wouldn't touch the case. In desperation, one of the customs house agents came to John Adams. Would he defend the soldiers and their officer?

Adams knew that his friends Sam Adams and John Hancock expected him to support the Sons of Liberty. In principle, he agreed with them about the rights of Massachusetts over the tyranny of the Crown. If he took the unpopular case it would foolishly risk his reputation, his legal practice, perhaps even his life. Boston would hate the man who defended the murderers of its sons.

He thought of his father. He even thought of the arguments between the deacon and Susanna over doing what was right—not what was easy or comfortable.

He didn't like the customs agent and he didn't know Captain Preston. Why should he help them? Weren't they the arm of tyranny?

But liberty couldn't be bought with tarnished principles. The principle of a fair trial for every man was holy to John Adams. That idea stood higher in his mind than the opinion of his friends or how he leaned toward a cause.

He paused a heartbeat or two, then nodded. He said, "A lawyer must hold himself accountable not only to his country but to God, who is the source of all justice. I will represent the accused without tricks or lies, with only the evidence of the case— no more than fact and the law will justify."

The agent grasped John's hand. "This is all Captain Preston requests of you: the law. As God almighty is my judge, Mr. Adams, I believe him an innocent man."

John replied, "If he thinks he cannot have a fair trial without my assistance, he shall have it without hesitation."

Paul Revere made John's job more difficult. The patriot and silversmith had immediately printed his engraving of "The Boston Massacre" showing Captain Preston with his sword leveled, ordering his men to fire on an orderly and innocent crowd. In the engraving, wounded and dying men already lay in the street. Boston's newspapers carried questionable eyewitness reports. The matter of guilt seemed settled.

Captain Preston was tried first. Adams, assisted by his friend and fellow-lawyer John Quincy (Colonel John Quincy's son), easily established that the scene was more disorderly than Revere depicted. It was louder and more confused. Could any witness swear that he had heard Captain Preston give the order to fire? No. All the evidence suggested that the soldiers had fired on their own, goaded by threats and fear, pelted by rocks and bricks. The jury deliberated only a few hours and acquitted Captain Preston.

The trial of the soldiers was more difficult. They had, after all, fired their muskets. Adams's experience showed in his selection of the jury. He excused jurymen from Boston, choosing instead farmers from the rural areas outside the city. He knew that these steady men distrusted the rabble of Boston as much as John did. He was satisfied that his clients stood before a fair-minded group of jurors.

The prosecution called passionate eyewitnesses who swore that the soldiers tumbled out of their barracks swearing vengeance on "the damned Yankees," and vowing to kill them all. These angry witnesses described the crowd as a chance collection of Bostonians out for a stroll in the moonlight, mown down by British muskets for revenge.

Adams and Quincy offered more believable, less frantic witnesses, who reported the crowd as angry, insulting, taunting. They described the things that were thrown, the fear of the soldiers, and the loud menace of the mob.

178

"Why is it," Adams asked the jury, "that we have heard the persons who swarmed at the soldiers called so many things—innocents, boys, strollers—but we haven't heard them called a mob? The plain English is, gentlemen, that they were a motley rabble of saucy boys, violent ruffians, and outlandish Jack Tars. Why should we scruple to call them a mob? I cannot tell, unless the name *mob* is too respectful for them.

"When the multitude was shouting and threatening life, the bells all ringing, the mob whistle screaming and rending like an Indian yell, the people from all quarters throwing every species of rubbish they could pick up in the street, and some who were quite on the other side of the street throwing clubs at the whole party, Montgomery in particular, smote with a club and knocked down, and as soon as he could rise and take up his firelock, another club from afar struck his breast or shoulder, what could he do? Do you expect he should behave like a Stoic Philosopher lost in apathy?

"It is impossible you should find him guilty of murder. You must suppose him [to be without feelings] if you don't think him at the least provoked, thrown off his guard, and [confused] by such treatment.

"Facts are stubborn things. Whatever may be our wishes, our inclinations, or the dictates of our passions, they cannot alter the state of facts and evidence. To your candor and justice I submit the prisoners and their cause.

"The law will preserve a steady course. It does not bend to the wishes, imaginations, and tempers of men. It does not lend itself to what pleases a weak, frail man, but without regard to persons it punishes evil in all, whether rich or poor, high or low. 'Tis deaf, unstoppable, inflexible. On the one hand it ignores the cries of prisoners; on the other it is deaf, deaf as a snake to the clamor of the populace."

The jury deliberated for several hours. It acquitted six of the soldiers. Two were judged guilty of simple manslaughter. These men were sentenced to dismissal from the armed forces, and to have their thumbs branded with a hot iron, so that they would carry a mark of shame forever.

There was some complaint in the Boston news-papers about John Adams's defense of the hated lobsterbacks, and even Sam Adams criticized him under his pen name "Vindex," but privately Sam respected John's integrity. There were no riots, and no mobs pursued him. Perhaps John Adams forced the people of Boston to face the truth that a mob was a dangerous beast, even in the cause of liberty.

As a mark of the respect John still had, he was elected as a member of the state legislature in the spring. He would fill the place left vacant when his hero James Otis became too mentally disturbed to continue.

John was one of the first suburban commuters. He traveled from Braintree to Boston almost daily. He dined with his cousin Samuel, took the ferry across to Cambridge for assembly meetings, and carried on a busy law practice. His brother Peter had married and now lived on his wife's farm, so John bought and added the original acres to his own farm. He read and wrote and played with the children (there were four of them now) and spent quality time with Abigail. It was a strenuous, active, fulfilling life. Still, that "interior" John Adams, the self-doubting voice within him, continued to nag. Though he rode hundreds of miles and worked with his hired men in the fields, he wrote in his diary that he was "sickly and weak, full of pain." He suspected many strange diseases and continued his diet of milk, vegetables, and toast, which may have been the cause of his frail feelings. He loved the clamor of Boston but wanted to be on his quiet marsh. He was strong as an ox but felt frail. He hated politics but needed to be part of it. John Adams was not a simple man but a stubborn, contradictory Swamp Yankee.

The Hall

John Adams was astonished by his own outburst! How could he have been so discourteous? It almost leaped out of his mouth. He was sitting at a dinner party with friends in Boston when a British guest began to praise the long history of British justice, the fairness of the British courts. . . .

"There is no more justice in Britain than in hell!" John exploded. "I could wish that the Bourbon king of France landed on England's back. Misfortune and disaster might bring England back to its senses and its sense of duty!" He rose and left, mumbling apologies to his host but not to the Briton.

"Perhaps," John said to Abigail, "my real feelings about this situation are not so logical and abstract as I thought. Perhaps my heart has made a decision that my mind has not yet reached."

Instead of soothing her colonists, Britain grew more rigid and less sensitive to colonial dignity.

Colonists had refused to buy many British products as a protest against the import taxes. Patriotic colonial housewives and tavern-keepers stopped buying tea. In 1773, the London warehouses of the British East India Company were overflowing with chests of tea meant for the colonies. As a favor to the important and influential company, Parliament allowed the oversupply of tea to be shipped to America without the normal export tax. Even with the import tax of three pence per pound paid in the colonies, the tea would be cheap. How could Americans refuse a bargain like that? They could. And they were gravely insulted. It was the same hateful tax, even if it was paid on cheap tea.

The merchant ships *Eleanor, Beaver,* and *Dartmouth* docked in Boston Harbor and prepared to offload 342 chests of tea. Sam Adams stood before an angry crowd at Faneuil Hall. "Are pennies more important than principles?" he shouted. Then, "I wonder how tea mixes with salt water?" At that moment, painted and disguised as Mohawk Indians, dozens of Liberty Boys ran past the windows of Faneuil Hall toward the dock. The crowd followed them. It wasn't a casual prank: The "Indians" were well-rehearsed and efficient. They posted sentries, took control of the ships, hauled the chests of tea up from the holds and dumped them into Boston Harbor.

John Adams heard about the "tea party" next morning. He didn't like mobs, but there was something charmingly symbolic about this exercise of public disgust. Dressing up as Indians gave the vandals a memorably distinct American character, and made the act more than simple sabotage. It was a message from the American continent to the Old World.

Could the British–American situation be saved? Letters were exchanged up and down the American coast. In 1774, it was decided that representatives from all the colonies would meet. Together, they might convince King George and Parliament that American anger and frustration didn't come from a nest of malcontents in a single colony but was a feeling held by honorable men throughout the colonies. This gathering called itself the First Continental Congress, and met at Carpenters' Hall in Philadelphia.

John Adams was one of the representatives chosen from Massachusetts. It was a fifteen-day ride from Braintree, the farthest he had ever been from his marsh.

Philadelphia was exciting—the largest city in the colonies and the most active seaport. It was more than twice as large as Boston and humming with ideas. It had seventeen newspapers and twenty-three printers. The spacious city, debate, friendships, and personalities fascinated John, even though he fiercely missed Abigail and their family. He wrote, often more than once a day. He lodged in Mrs. Sarah Yard's boarding house near the hall for months. But when he returned to Braintree in August, the Continental Congress hadn't made a wrinkle in British policy. Time had run out for a reconciliation between the mother country and her daughter colonies.

On April 19, 1775, a regiment of British redcoats prepared for a secret march from Boston to Concord, about twenty miles inland. A British loyalist had reported that the Massachusetts militia kept a large supply of gunpowder there. Lt. Colonel Francis Smith had orders to seize the powder.

But every British movement in Boston was watched. The longboats ferrying Smith's regiment across the Charles River were reported, and two riders, the silversmith Paul Revere and William Dawes, rode through the country ahead of the British, alerting town militias. On the Lexington commons Smith's columns confronted a band of "minutemen," the colonial militia. These were militia soldiers who had promised to keep their rifles and powder horns close enough to be ready for a fight in less than a minute. The two groups fired on one another briefly. A few Lexington men were killed but the rest disappeared into the brush. The regiment marched on for Concord. When they started into Concord on the narrow North Bridge, they were repelled by heavy rifle fire from the minutemen. Smith quickly realized he was surrounded. His position was dangerous and he ordered a retreat toward Boston. The redcoats' retreat was their real battle. Minutemen fired into the orderly British ranks from both sides of the road, mile after mile, picking off one redcoat after another. When the regiment was saved by a British relief column it had lost nearly forty percent of its soldiers.

The colonies were now in armed revolution against Britain, and Boston was under siege. Massachusetts militia, reinforced by militiamen from other states, surrounded the British in the town and the harbor. At the Adams farm Abigail and the children were relatively safe, though the Braintree militia turned out when British boats approached Weymouth and tried to carry off a few tons of hay from Grape Island. The British were beaten off and their fodder burned. Abigail wrote to John in Philadelphia, "Soldiers continually pass our farm on the Coast Road, to and from our lines at Boston. Some stop for a drink of cider or a meal. Many times the parlor floor is covered with tired soldiers or refugees from the siege, weary and shaken."

Their flow of letters was a lifeline to both of them. Abigail wrote, "Spend more time with me through your pen, John. Your letters are written in so much haste that they scarcely leave room for social feelings. Some are not more than six lines long. They are often more like dispatches from the battlefront than comforts to your devoted wife. Perhaps the debates of Congress are secret, but please share with me the sentimental secrets of your heart. I am sure you have them," she teased, "if they are not all absorbed by the great public."

Two months after the Battle of Concord, the Massachusetts militia made another surprise move. In a single night they marched from the north and built defenses on Breed's Hill, next to Bunker Hill, above Charlestown, a short way across the inlet from Boston. The British sent a landing force of 2400 soldiers against the 1500 militiamen. The redcoats, under General William Howe, landed in barges and formed up for a charge. Could the untrained, undisciplined colonial militia stand up to the finest assault troops in the world? The militia troops were outnumbered and parts of their force had only thirty musket balls per man. Colonel Prescott, their leader, told them to make each ball count—"Don't fire until you see the whites of their eyes!"

The British charged twice and were beaten back with terrible losses. Redcoats regrouped at the base of Breed's Hill and attacked again. This time the Americans melted away in an orderly and well-timed retreat. The British had won a technical victory but had lost over one thousand men, some killed and some wounded. The Americans had four hundred dead and wounded. The real outcome of the Battle of Bunker Hill was that American militiamen proved they could beat the British toe to toe. General Howe said, "It was a dear-bought victory. Another such victory would have ruined us."

In 1776, the Second Continental Congress had moved from Carpenters' Hall to Town Hall, and the harmony of the delegates had changed too.

John wrote to Abigail, "I fear there will be a North and a South party in Congress, tearing all our work to pieces. I, myself, nominated General Washington, a Virginian, as commander of the army when John Hancock wanted the post. Still, the southern gentlemen suspect that Massachusetts and the New England colonies are full of plans for our own benefit. Now we receive—too late!—a plea from Parliament and Lord North, promising that we will have no further duty, taxes, or assessments levied on us. Ha! North thinks he can sing a lullaby so the innocent children will go to sleep. He wants us to delay, debate, and diddle, hoping for more concessions from Parliament. When will we declare our real independence?"

John saw once-dedicated leaders wavering. He wrote Abigail a letter about one of them. "My weak-minded friend John Dickinson has wiggled out of his convictions. I find that he is whispering with the delegates of South Carolina, asking them to oppose any measure that leads to a final break with the Mother Country. South Carolina is already a difficult opponent of clear action against Fat King George. Dickinson heads the Cool Men, the minority against independence. He authored the wicked 'Olive Branch Petition,' asking Britain to be kind, so we could return to their arms. Yes, I signed the Petition, but only because it served a real purpose: If Fat George and Parliament rejected it, then our minority would be more receptive to independence. We sent two copies of the document in separate ships. Both arrived and George would read neither. There's Dickinson's answer! And why this change of principle in a good man like Dickinson? Because his wife and his mother have told him, 'Johnny, you will be hanged, your estate will be confiscated, and you will leave your excellent wife a widow, your children will be orphans, beggars, . . .' Fish and fowl! If I had such a mother and such a wife, I would have shot myself!"

It was a shocking blow to the harmony of Congress that this letter was intercepted by British agents and published in newspapers. John Adams's reputation for wise deliberation was blemished. Many members of Congress avoided him now, and Dickinson would no longer speak to him.

For once, he was impervious to opinion. John ignored snubs and scorn and kept pressing for action. He chided the delegates, "The middle way is no way at all. If we finally fail in this great and glorious contest, it will be by bewildering ourselves in groping for the middle way!"

He was now totally convinced that there had to be a complete break with Britain. He stubbornly infuriated every man in Congress with his impatience and continuous argument in favor of independence. A new delegate, arriving late from Virginia, would be his firmest ally in that argument and become a lifelong friend—as well as John's bitterest political rival. No two men in Congress were less alike than John Adams and Thomas Jefferson.

Thomas Jefferson was from Virginia, the oldest and most respected of the colonies. He was tall and slim, six feet and three inches, standing a head taller than plump John Adams's five feet and four inches. Jefferson had thick red hair and freckles, long hands and huge feet; he stood quietly aloof, often with his hands folded almost defensively across his broad chest. John Adams was small, light on his tiny feet, nearly always in motion, and seemed almost aggressive in the way he talked to people so closely.

Jefferson had few friends and was distant to the people around him, but had an almost reverent respect for "the people." Adams cherished many close friends, dealt intimately with people, but mistrusted "the mob." In a debate, Jefferson was soft-spoken, distant, and calculating, content to allow others whatever beliefs they chose. Adams was a terrier, loudly challenging any opinion that seemed wrong.

Jefferson was a man of refined tastes, a musician, architect, scientist, inventor, and geographer. Adams was a charming but blunt Swamp Yankee who chewed tobacco and took his rum straight.

Thomas Jefferson was a Virginia aristocrat,

come to Congress from his vast and elegant estate, Monticello, worked by hundreds of slaves. Adams was a man of regular income and Spartan tastes who worked in the fields with his hired help.

And yet in their hearts they were much alike, passionate and principled. Few men in Congress, the cream of the colonies, were as learned and widely read as Jefferson and Adams. Both were stamped indelibly by the land they came from. Adams was forty-one, Jefferson was thirty-three. The younger man was like a respectful younger brother; he admired Adams, appreciated his energy and will, and asked for his advice. Both men were wholly devoted to the cause of an American nation independent of Britain.

Both Adams and Jefferson asked for a clean break from Britain, a decisive statement that would declare themselves a new nation rather than a pack of rebel colonies. The cautious delegates asked, "What would this resolution say?" A committee was formed to construct a statement: John Adams (Massachusetts), Thomas Jefferson (Virginia), Benjamin Franklin (Pennsylvania), Roger Sherman

(Connecticut), and Robert Livingston (New York). Jefferson suggested that Adams write the statement.

"No, Jefferson, you must do it."

"Why?" he asked mildly.

"Reasons enough."

"What can be your reasons?"

"Reason first: You are a Virginian and a Virginian ought to appear at the head of this business. Reason second: I am obnoxious, suspected, and unpopular. You are very much otherwise. Reason third: You can write ten times better than I can."

John was being too modest. He was a fine writer but, as he wrote to Abigail, "Jefferson has a particular felicity of expression."

The result was the Declaration of Independence. The document was not entirely original; it borrowed phrases and terms from many sources in America and Britain. But it had a particular felicity of expression, and a meaning so clear and simple that it set imaginations on fire.

Even so, the debate was long and bitter.

The declaration was changed in some ways. The anti-slavery provision was taken out. All thirteen colonies kept and profited from slaves (some said that half of Massachusetts's merchant vessels were involved in the slave trade). John Adams wanted slavery abolished but agreed to the cut saying, "Slavery cannot stand in the way of independence. First one, then the other." One of Jefferson's most tender phrases was removed: "We might have been a free and great people together." The debate raged, flamed, and shook hearts for nine hours.

On the second day of July, the resolution of independence from Britain was passed unanimously. It was announced and published on July 4, 1776.

New Jersey's delegate Richard Stockton said later of John Adams, "I call him the Atlas of the American independence. He it was who sustained the debate, and by the force of his reasoning demonstrated not only the justice, but the expediency of the measure."

The Commonwealth

John Adams had a price on his head. As one of the
loudest and most insistent advocates of independence, he led the list of condemned rebels. He was
in danger every time he rode outside Philadelphia,
where armed bands of Tories (British sympathizers) might hang him on the spot or spirit him away
to General Howe, still cruising up and down the
coast between the Chesapeake and New York.

Hopes for independence were sometimes frail.
It was unlikely that even half the population of the
colonies favored the break from Britain, the
strongest nation in the world. If General Washington
and the Continental Army lost this struggle, John

Adams was a rebel. In the unlikely event that the united colonies might win, he was a patriot. It seemed possible that the life of these new United States of America might be brief.

He remembered his pride in British citizenship. He thought of the affection he had felt for the British Army officers Braintree had entertained as they passed through on their way to the front during the French and Indian War. He remembered General Washington admitting to him that his highest aspiration as a young militia commander was to be an officer of the King's Army.

Philadelphia was as hot as a furnace in the summer of 1777. John nourished himself with small pleasures like dining at Mrs. Cheesman's, the jolly boarding house where Sam Adams and Roger Sherman lived. He always found good food, jokes, gossip, and healing laughter there. In his own quiet rooms, John was working on organization and supply details for General Washington's barely trained army. He wrote directions and guidelines for the almost-laughable navy—until thirteen new frigates were launched, the United States Navy had only a few tiny gunboats and a handful of privateers. His greatest solace was in the letters that traveled so slowly between Philadelphia and Braintree.

Awed by the sight of soldiers marching past the Adams farm, young Tommy Adams wanted to become a general. His father wrote, "I believe I must make a physician of you. Would it please you to study nature and to relieve your fellow creatures of pain and distress? Is this not better than destroying mankind by the thousands? You could change your title from 'General Tommy' to 'Doctor Tommy.' Generals must be brave and strong to care for an army, but being a doctor requires a rugged and tough character, riding and walking night and day to visit the sick."

In July 1777, Abigail gave birth to a stillborn daughter. She wrote to her husband, "I dreamed of presenting you with a fine son or daughter, and of your look of delight. But these dreams are buried in the infant's grave, transitory as the morning cloud. If you will come home and turn farmer, I will be a dairy woman and we will grow wealthy."

John wrote, "Three years of service to my land have been tedious and demanding beyond description. What have I not suffered? What have I not hazarded? Let the cymbals of popularity tinkle still. Let the butterflies of fame glitter with their wings. I shall envy neither their music nor their colors. I am condemned to the dullest servitude and drudgery, separated from all that I love. Digging in my own potato garden would be to me a paradise."

There was a rumor that General Howe was sailing down the coast to the mouth of the Delaware to attack Philadelphia. John reassured Abigail, "If Howe comes here I shall run away, I suppose, with the rest of Congress. We are too brittle, you know, to stand the dashing of balls and bombs. During the sack of Rome, its senators preferred to be put to the sword rather than fly from the invading Gauls. We do not intend to indulge this sort of dignity."

General Howe came up the Delaware River in September. John Adams reported to Abigail, "We scurried out of Philadelphia, chased like a covey of partridges!"

But the news wasn't all bad. The British commander in the north, Gentleman Johnny Burgoyne, had surrendered his army to American Major General Horatio Gates at Saratoga. In October, with winter coming on, most of Congress returned to their homes.

The United States of America desperately needed an ally. With European military support the new nation might wear down the British forces. With European loans it might buy guns, shot, gunpowder, artillery pieces, and other stores not yet manufactured in America. Congress had great hopes that France might recognize and finance the United States, but the delegation they had sent was having difficulty. Someone, a man of will and sense, had to sort the situation out. Against Abigail's tears and protests, John Adams and his ten-year-old son, John Quincy Adams, boarded a longboat on the icy beach in front of the Adams's marsh in February 1778. They set out for France aboard the new, Massachusetts-built, United States Navy frigate *Boston*, into the teeth of the North Atlantic winter gales.

It was a six-week passage through storms and danger. Early in the voyage, a fleet of three Royal Navy vessels sighted and chased *Boston*. Captain Samuel Tucker was a Marblehead, Massachusetts, sailor raised on the water. He quickly left two of the British frigates far behind. For a few minutes he considered doubling back and engaging the third frigate, broadside to broadside. He was sure his twenty-four-gun ship could take the pounding and give better than she got. But his orders were clear: deliver John Adams to France without delay. He outdistanced the last frigate and drove hard for France.

Boston sighted a British armed merchantman. It was a small ship, not a serious threat, so Captain Tucker gave chase. Within a few hours they were close enough for long shots from their cannon. *Boston* fired her bow chaser. The merchantman fired her stern chaser and shattered *Boston's* mizzen yard (the wooden support for the aftermost sail). Tucker ducked his head at the explosion, then looked back to see if anyone was wounded by flying splinters. Directly under the mizzen sail he saw John Adams priming his musket in the ranks of *Boston*'s soldiers, ready for the fight. *Boston* came closer to the merchantman, then turned in preparation for a broadside. The merchantman— *Martha,* out of London—surrendered as soon as she saw *Boston*'s long row of gunports.

In the bustle of taking over *Martha* as a prize, Captain Tucker found Adams and his musket among the soldiers again. "What are you doing here, sir?"

Adams replied simply, "I ought to do my share of the fighting."

The Navy Board asked Captain Tucker later, about his passage with John Adams. "I didn't say much to him at first, but damn and blast my eyes, after a while I found him as sociable as any damned Marblehead man."

John and Johnny went ashore at Bordeaux, France, on April 1, 1778.

John loved and hated France.

He was enchanted by the people, their manners, the landscape, the food, the architecture.

Every day was a delight. Paris was one of the two or three largest cities in the world and he had so much to learn. He could not yet speak French with any ease, and yet people everywhere were so patient and hospitable.

He was also uneasy with the ease of French life, their love of decoration and parties and fancy dress. He suspected their morals must be as loose as their easygoing taste for luxury. As a man of republican virtue, he loved, but disapproved of, French culture.

He was especially impressed with the women of France. They were more beautiful in dress and style than any women he had encountered, but they were also well educated, intelligent, and bold. They did not allow men to dominate conversations but declared and defended their opinions with equal conviction. John liked strong, intelligent women; they reminded him of Abigail.

John discovered one of the problems with the French delegation immediately. The two primary members were Benjamin Franklin and Arthur Lee. They hated one another. Lee hated Franklin so much that he refused to live in the same town, and moved to a small village nearby.

Franklin was the darling of France, and probably the best-known man in the world. He was famous and wealthy because of *Poor Richard's Almanack*, but he was equally famous as a scientist. The invention of the lightning rod, alone, would have established his credentials, but he had gone on to define the properties of electricity, to map the Gulf Stream, and to perform many other original experiments. He was celebrated as a social reformer—the man who founded the first American scientific society, firefighting company, library, hospital, and medical school. He was a philanthropist, musician, writer, wit, and sage. His face appeared everywhere—on tin trays, medals, buttons, rugs, mugs, and even, it was rumored, painted inside chamber pots for the royalty. He was welcome at every party, dressed in his slightly theatrical "homespun American" clothing, with his bear-fur hat and fur-collared jacket. Adams, who was learning French rapidly, discovered that Franklin spoke French very poorly. Even this added to his popularity; Parisians thought it was amusing.

Both men made Adams frantic with impatience. He discovered that the treaty of French support for which he had been sent was already signed. There was an enormous amount of organizational work to do, however, and neither Franklin nor Lee were suited to the job. Franklin was elderly, attended late-night parties, indulged himself in wine and food, and suffered from gout. He rose no earlier than ten o'clock. Lee was not an energetic man, and by the time he rose and dressed and arrived at the house in which Franklin and Adams lived and worked, it was eleven o'clock. Franklin insisted on leaving for lunch and social calls at two. Lee would often leave in anger before then.

Adams rose each morning at five and began his paperwork. He tried to soothe the anger between the two strange men to no avail. Adams worked long, difficult days, performing an amazing labor in adjusting the accounts of the delegation— neither Franklin nor Lee had kept records of expenses.

The almost insurmountable difficulty of such a delegation was the vast space between Paris and America. To send a proposal or question to Congress in Philadelphia and receive a reply often took six months! Adams wrote to Congress, recommending that a single person, Franklin, be in charge of the delegation, to dispense with additional difficulties of argument and disagreement.

On March 8, 1779, John and John Quincy Adams left Paris.

On August 2, 1779, a boat from the French frigate *La Sensible* rowed John and John Quincy ashore, depositing them on the beach within strolling distance of the Adams home. They had been gone for a year and a half.

John Adams had sacrificed much for his country and his beliefs. He had been the strongest, the most persuasive, and the most persistent voice for independence and liberty. He had performed great things and a great number of small things as a member of the Congress and its committees. But his most enduring contribution to his country was just beginning. John Adams and others in Congress had encouraged the thirteen states to create the form of their internal governments as quickly as possible, to present an orderly federation of democratic states to the world. In September, enjoying the smell of his own marsh and the taste of his own cider again, John was elected to the Massachusetts Assembly Commission to form a system of government. He returned from Boston the next day.

"What are ye doing with the Assembly, John?" Abigail asked him as she fixed supper.

"We are laying out the parts of Massachusetts's government, its functions and its rules of motion."

"And who is working with you?"

John smiled into his mug of hard cider with satisfaction, "I seem to be a sub-sub-committee of one, my dear."

He had been thinking about this problem for several years: *"A just government must be a government of laws, not of men. And it must be balanced within itself, so that no one arm of government can seize the selfish powers of a king or the mindless powers of a mob."*

Years of this thought and all his powers of logic bubbled in his mind. He visited his brother-in-law Richard Cranch and watched him assemble the parts of a large steeple clock. He mused on the power of the pendulum's weight to regulate the pace, the power of the escapement to communicate the tick of time, and the power of the gears to drive the hands for minutes and hours. No one power was more important than another. It was a clockwork of checks and balances.

What would a rational state, a device to share the fortunes of men, be called? He called it a "commonwealth."

He began "A Constitution or Form of Government for the Commonwealth of Massachusetts," with a preamble laying out the need for rules and what the people of Massachusetts hoped to accomplish with the rules.

He went on to a declaration of rights; these were rights that every citizen of the commonwealth shared. He wrote, "All men are born equally free and independent," as a basis for the rights. The Massachusetts Assembly changed this

to "All men are born equal and free." John disagreed because he knew that all men were not
equal. Some were more powerful, more eloquent,
or more intelligent than others, but all men were
born equally free.

Citizens of the commonwealth had a right to free
elections, freedom of speaking, and liberty of the
press. They had freedom from the kind of unrea-
sonable searches and seizures the writs of assistance had made possible. A citizen accused of a
crime had a right to a trial by jury, not merely
judgement by an appointed figure.

"No one," he wrote, remembering his Puritan
ancestors fleeing Bloody Mary, "shall be hurt,
molested, or restrained in his person, liberty, or
estate for worshipping God in the manner most
agreeable to the dictates of his own conscience."

An entirely new concept appeared in Adams's
constitution. It was an idea peculiar to the new
world of America and made a clear break with
Europe's governments. "No one has advantage
or privilege except what arises from considera-
tion of services rendered to the public." Adams's

constitution forbade hereditary titles, noble families, and ancestral privileges. "The idea of a man being born a magistrate, lawgiver, or judge is absurd and unnatural."

To direct the commonwealth, Adams created a clockwork mechanism of three parts: "The legislative, executive, and judicial power shall be placed in separate departments, to the end that it might be a government of laws, and not of men." Each department was separate and balanced. No department had complete control over another, and each department had some way to prevent the others from straying too far. Adams also balanced the rights of the population against the rights of districts regardless of their population by separating the legislative branch into two separate parts. In the House of Representatives, each district had a number of representative votes proportional to their population; in the Senate, each district had an equal vote.

Finally, John Adams added a far-sighted encouragement to the constitution, a legacy of his Puritan belief that independence of thought was possible only in an educated congregation. It was also a product of John's love for books, his admiration for men of science, and his pleasure in life. "It is the duty of government to provide education and cherish the interests of literature and science, including the whole range of the arts." He dedicated the commonwealth to advocating the virtues of charity, activity, thrift, honesty, sincerity, virtue, and even amiability.

The Massachusetts Assembly adopted John's constitution in almost every detail. They even adopted his title, commonwealth, for the state. The liberty of the press was dropped for a time but later reinstated. The Constitution of the Commonwealth of Massachusetts was so clear and logical that it became the model for the Constitution of the United States. It is one of the significant documents of the American Revolution and is John Adams's perennial gift to his country.

The President's House

John Adams didn't fit. The honest, blunt Yankee farmer was prepared to argue with neighbors or tyrants, or to take his musket and join the melee of a battle at sea. But he was unprepared and unsuited to the smiling, secret struggles of diplomacy and politics. He was, like Massachusetts quahog chowder, an acquired taste. Many people didn't like their first spoonful of John Adams—too salty and natural, too assertive, too much a part of the sea and the land, and not enough of the parlor and dinner table.

He hadn't been home for three months before Congress sent him back to France to negotiate for a possible peace with Britain. This time he took two sons, John Quincy and Charlie. Abigail grieved but encouraged Johnny to go with his father for the sights and experience. "Rivers grow broader and deeper the farther they flow from their source," she assured him—though she had never been farther than a day's ride from her childhood home.

The sights and tastes of Paris were just as agreeable to John as before, but the situation was not. He announced his mission to France's Foreign Minister, the Comte de Vergennes, and was stopped in his tracks. The Minister insisted that it was unwise for Adams to reveal his peacemaking purpose, and Benjamin Franklin agreed. John was shocked: Why not? Had the United States declared independence to be ruled by French noblemen? He insisted. He wrote stacks of letters. He criticized Franklin: "You live too much like one of these pleasure-loving Frenchmen. You've lost your American edge. They are a crowd of backstairs schemers and dawdlers, smiling while they try to take the rug from under us. Yes, we should be grateful to the French, but we must keep our dignity and our independence!"

The French minister led John into an argument and used it as an excuse to have Adams separated from official diplomacy. Franklin sent Congress a note criticizing Adams as a diplomat. Hopping mad, with no real duties to occupy him, John packed up his sons and his household and clattered off to the Netherlands.

It was a kind of pilgrimage since John's Puritan ancestors had found refuge there against religious intolerance in England before they sailed for America. In Amsterdam, acting as a private citizen and without the approval of Congress, he tried to persuade the Dutch to officially recognize the United States as a nation, and to arrange much-needed national loans from Dutch banks.

He put the boys into Amsterdam's Latin School, but they didn't speak the cumbersome language and were placed in classes with much younger children. The schoolmaster penned a note to their father: "Both these boys are proud and vain. They cause great irritation and will not submit them-

216

selves to the proper conduct of the classroom. Fear not: We will thrash them into submission. A touch of the cane does wonders for stubborn boys."

Schoolmaster Cleverly leaped unpleasantly to John's mind. "Sir," came the immediate reply, "please send my boys home to me this evening."

The boys were tutored in their new home but Charlie was as attached to the Braintree marsh as his father had been, and was desperately homesick for his mother. John sent Charlie home with his tutor in an American ship, longing to return with him but held in Holland by the possibility of winning European help in America's crisis.

He placed such trust in John Quincy that he sent him on a critically important diplomatic mission. The fourteen year old spoke French so well, was so bright, and had such a gift for dealing gracefully with people that he was made interpreter for the American delegation to the court of Russia. He traveled twelve hundred miles to a strange capital in a strange empire that few Americans had ever seen. It was plain that John and Abigail were training the boy for a life of service to his country.

John wrote to a friend, "Though I love the art I see all about me in Europe, I would not educate my sons in the fine arts. I study politics and war that my sons may have liberty to study mathematics and philosophy. My sons ought to study mathematics and philosophy, geography, natural history, naval architecture, navigation, commerce, and agriculture in order to give their children a right to study painting, poetry, music, architecture, statuary, tapestry, and porcelain." But John Quincy Adams would, like his father, study politics and war.

For once John felt like Abigail, who tried to ignore her own sadness when she sent her loved ones away. Looking down on the canal in Amsterdam, so far from his marsh, he reflected, "I consented [to send my boys away] . . . and thus deprived myself of the greatest pleasure I had in life."

The time in the Netherlands without his sons was hard on John Adams. He contracted a fever— malaria or typhus—and nearly died. But when he was strong enough to hold a pen, he wrote. He produced a great storm of letters to Congress, political friends, and Dutch leaders. He wrote a series of articles about America and its cause for the Dutch press, creating popular support for the United States of America.

Across the Atlantic, something like a miracle occurred. General Washington's Continental Army, with help from French General Rochambeau's troops, had bottled up the British. In the autumn of 1781, General Cornwallis and his British army were defending themselves behind weary lines of defense at Yorktown, Virginia, when Admiral de Grasse sailed into the mouth of Chesapeake Bay with a powerful French fleet. Cornwallis surrendered his army of seven thousand troops.

When the news reached London, the British Prime Minister cried, "Oh God! It's all over!"

America's struggle wasn't entirely over.

This recent *"Cornwallization* will well warrant," John wrote, "a higher tone" of pursuit of a Dutch loan. John's time and effort in Holland bore fruit—

in 1782 the Dutch recognized the United States of America as an independent nation, and Adams wangled a $2,000,000 loan from bankers in Amsterdam.

There were long, difficult negotiations for a peace treaty. Delicate diplomacy was required in some discussions. In others, America needed a terrier again. John Adams returned to Paris and doggedly argued the British into useful agreements on fishing rights along the Canadian coast. With farsighted concern about the United States's expansion west, Adams convinced the British to cede all the territory between the Appalachians and the Mississippi River. This single agreement doubled the size of the new nation.

With the Treaty of Paris, September 3, 1783, the American Revolution was over. John and John Quincy toured Britain, and John received an appointment from Congress as the first United States Minister to Britain.

Despite her terror of the ocean, Abigail agreed to join John in Paris on the way to Britain. After months of preparation, Abigail and Nabby Adams, with two servants and a cow, boarded the merchant vessel *Active* in Boston on June 20, 1784, and sailed off into the Atlantic Ocean to join John after three years of separation.

John Adams still didn't fit the diplomatic model of polite distance, agreeable disagreement, and secret bargains. He was simply too honest and plainspoken for the job. The Adams family spent three pleasant but unsuccessful years in London and left without establishing better trade relations or improving British opinion of the "upstart colonies."

During that time, however, John was busy writing a three-volume discussion of government structure. He described and expanded on his constitution for Massachusetts, explained the theory of checks and balances, and stressed the dangers of any one branch of government holding unchecked power over the others. Though he believed that the individual states had independent powers, he worried about the strength of the central government to hold them together, and attempted in his book to bring together the interests of the states and of the union. His book was consulted daily during the Constitutional Convention of 1787. It was a powerful influence in creating a lasting document, and a lasting union.

He longed for his marsh and the smell of Massachusetts Bay. In 1788 he resigned as minister to Britain and returned to Braintree. John Adams was deep in the marsh mud and the good manure from Adams livestock soon after the family landed in Boston.

Disaster. In the first national election, not a year after John returned home, George Washington was elected President of the United States—and John was elected Vice President!

It was not a position he could conceivably refuse. He would be part of the government he had, in large part, designed. And so he left his marsh again for the new capital in New York City, and a job that had only a few official duties. Among those was the Vice President's position as president of the Senate. He moderated debate, helped to ease the flow of argument, and often cast the

deciding vote to break a deadlock. His vote always went toward strengthening the central government. John's contrary nature affected his reputation with the Senate, and even with President Washington, when he advocated calling the head of the nation, "His Majesty, the President." Perhaps he wanted only to put the presidency on the same high footing as the kings of other nations ,but his colleagues began to suspect him of being a secret monarchist.

On July 14, 1789, a mob in Paris stormed the royal prison, the Bastille. The French Revolution had begun. It had little in common with the American Revolution. The colonies of America had declared themselves an independent state; France was an independent state rebelling against an existing government. America's independence was a step toward a rational, lasting democratic government; France's revolt was a bitter reaction to the excesses of monarchy, and how its chosen "republican" government failed to represent all of France's citizens.

There was another shocking difference. After

the American Revolution there were virtually no reprisals or punishments against supporters of Britain. The events of the French Revolution were bloody. Each new ship from France brought horrible news. On August 10, 1792, a radical mob slaughtered six hundred royal Swiss guards where King Louis XVI and his family were being held. Louis was beheaded on January 21, 1793.

The French Revolution and the wave of violence it included stirred the cauldron of young American politics to a dangerous fury. After all, it was the monarchy of France under Louis XVI that had made American independence possible.

But hadn't America declared itself free of monarchies and noble titles? Weren't France and America united in this refusal to abide by old lies?

There was also the guilty knowledge that France's enormous expenditures of military aid to the American Revolution had nearly bankrupt the French treasury and had, in some part, caused the French Revolution.

John was cautious about compromising the position of vice president. He remained silent and would not comment publicly on what he saw as plain animal ferocity, a pack of dogs unleashed.

John's old friend Jefferson, for years the United States minister to France and a great advocate of French culture, saw their Revolution as necessary and correct. He had known and liked Louis XVI, yet he responded to news of his beheading by saying, "Reason and liberty are overspreading the world. . . . Monarchy and autocracy must be annihilated and the rights of the people firmly established."

By 1793 the French Revolution had become the Reign of Terror. In Paris, alone, the guillotine accounted for three thousand aristocrats and their sympathizers. In the provinces, the slaughter was less humane. The city of Lyon rounded up hundreds and disposed of them with cannon fire. In Nantes, over three thousand "guilty" citizens were tied onto barges, which were sunk in the Loire River. Very few who died in the Terror carried much more guilt than a sense of tradition.

George Washington gravely and politely received Citizen Genét, minister to the United States from

France, and declared the neutrality of the United States, even though Revolutionary France was at war with every nation.

After two terms as president, George Washington was eager to retire. John Adams was his logical successor. But there was another new spoon whipping up American politics—party loyalties.

Both Washington and Adams despised political parties as dangerous and dividing. Two party factions, however, were clear: Federalists advocated a strong central government; Republicans wanted control in the hands of individual states. Jefferson was a skillful politician and schemer, the leader of the Republican party, and wanted the people to control the dangerous excesses of government. Adams wanted no part of a party, was a reluctant and unskillful politician, and wanted the government to control the dangerous impulses of the people. A monumental struggle between two good friends was approaching.

In 1794 John Jay returned from Britain after an exhausting effort to establish a working connection between Britain and the United States.

Revolutionary France and England were now officially at war. At the time, Jay's was the best treaty that could be expected. The fight for official approval of the treaty fractured Congress—Federalists were pro-British and for the Jay Treaty; Republicans were pro-French and against it.

John Quincy, to his father's vast pride, had recently been appointed the diplomatic representative to the Netherlands. Adams wrote to his twenty-seven-year-old son across the Atlantic, counseling him in the duties he might someday perform: "Johnny, I've got to stay out of this squabble. An executive official like the Vice President has a duty to remain neutral. Only then can he moderate the discussion between factions. This was my function when I presided over an arguing Senate. Alexander Hamilton, Washington's aide during the war, is now the leader of the Federalist party. I know he considers me one of them, and my sympathies, generally, are with their central-government ideas. But I do not have the right (or the desire) to be part of their party schemes. There is talk that Hamilton will try to replace me in the election with a 'loyal' Federalist. I cannot believe that he will forget my services to the country."

In the election of 1796, John's distance from the squabble over the Jay Treaty actually helped him. Moderate members of Congress stood with Adams and he was elected by a narrow margin of three electoral votes, even though Hamilton did try to undermine Adams with another candidate.

In early Presidential elections, president and vice president were not one ticket. The vice president was the candidate who received the second-highest number of electoral votes. John Adams's vice president was Thomas Jefferson, his personal friend, fellow farmer, and political rival.

Since John was the first president to follow another, there was no customary way to appoint a new cabinet of advisors. Adams tried to reconcile the Federalists and reassure the nation by keeping Washington's cabinet secretaries. But they were Federalists dedicated to Alexander Hamilton's faction, and began to work against Adams's policies immediately and secretly.

As a man of principle, John Adams couldn't fit

into politics. He tried to maintain a balance between parties and ideas within the government, appointing Republicans to important jobs (which angered the Federalists) and taking advice from his Federalist cabinet members (which angered the Republicans). He often associated with old friends who were now Republicans. John Adams enjoyed the political arguments. Hamilton and his cronies saw this as consorting with the enemy.

The resentment of France to America's neutrality and the Jay Treaty grew to a dangerous level. The French sent away the American diplomatic representative, and French privateers began to seize American vessels. The fledgling nation was threatened with a second war.

Republicans complained, "Why don't you assure the French of our support in their struggle against the British monarchy?"

Federalists nagged, "Why don't you declare war on these revolutionary barbarians?"

John did neither. Instead, he sent a carefully chosen delegation to seek peace with the French, headed by Charles Pinckney. The French foreign minister at first refused to meet the delegation, but then sent three agents—later known as "Monsieurs X, Y, and Z"—with a proposition. If the United States paid a large bribe to the minister and financed a loan for France, talks might begin. Pinckney was outraged, and shouted, "No! No! Not a sixpence!"

The delegation returned to Philadelphia where the government would meet until the new capital on the Potomac was prepared. John Adams tried to keep "The XYZ Affair" quiet so that a calm debate could settle things. But the Federalists leaked the facts to the press. Congress and the public were outraged, and the national cry was, "Millions for defense, but not a cent for tribute!"

Adams asked for funds from Congress to create a more powerful United States Navy and make the country ready for war. "This," he said to a friend, "is the carrot and the stick that may make this stubborn French mule move in the right direction. We hold the carrot of amiable peace in this hand, and the stick of a strong navy in the other. I'll tell you the truth, though: We could never strengthen our navy in time to make a difference. The navy is a bluff, but we'll keep a straight face while we're making that bluff. And in any case, this country needs a strong navy as soon as it can have one. The important thing is to let the French know that we will not back down. We will not be humiliated. The governments of the world will not deal fairly with us until we prove that we are prepared to fight for our rights."

Federalists were eager for war. Alexander Hamilton had schemed to have himself made inspector general of the United States forces under General Washington. Since Washington was too old to actually go into the field, Hamilton was effectively the military leader. He and many other party members wanted war with France to spread into Latin America as a springboard for expansion.

But a few armed merchantmen and United States Navy frigates had outgunned and out-sailed French privateers in the Atlantic. Their victories and Adams's bluff worked. The French recognized that the United States was willing to fight, and that was enough to send them to the bargaining table. Adams had established better relations and profitable trade with France without a war, which might have been disastrous to a young country.

John Adams's presidency was troubled by betrayal within his cabinet and angry party politics. It was also troubled by differing American views on the French Revolution and by simple growing pains. By trying to be fair and balanced in his position, he had made enemies on all sides. He was called a coward for avoiding war. He was called a fool for trusting friends. He was called a tyrant for signing the Alien and Sedition Acts that limited free speech and dissent.

Hamilton worked actively against Adams in the election of 1800. Because Federalist votes were split, Adams was defeated by Thomas Jefferson. He left office bitterly depressed that his country had given back so little of the love and energy he had offered.

John and Abigail spent a few months as the first residents of the unfinished President's House (which we now call the White House) before he left office. Abigail did her own laundry and hung it to dry in some of the big, empty rooms. John departed for Braintree early on the day of Thomas Jefferson's inauguration, before the ceremony, because he was too hurt to attend. While living in the house that still smelled of fresh cut wood and wet paint, he wrote to Abigail:

PRESIDENT'S HOUSE
WASHINGTON CITY
NOVEMBER 2, 1800

I pray Heaven to bestow the best of Blessings on this House and all that shall hereafter inhabit. May none but honest and wise men ever rule under this roof.

The Marsh

John Adams was home. The bitterness he had carried from the city of Washington and its scheming politicians was black and heavy. But it dropped away as he threw himself into the work of the farm.

Former President Adams was sixty-six. Fat and fit and strong, he was usually covered with dust or mud or manure as he worked alongside his hired men. The weather was fortunate and he looked toward a grand harvest. There was so much to do on the Adams farm, and he planned his improvements with glee he couldn't hide.

Like his father, John had added to his farm, acre by acre. He called it Stoneyfield now, his little joke about the stone-filled Massachusetts land. It had grown to six hundred acres of fields, woods, and salt marshes. He tended it joyfully, but he was a serious farmer. His service to the country had left him with little except this land—which, as the deacon would have said, hadn't broken or run away. But it was supporting a much larger family now.

John's son Charles had died, so his wife and two daughters lived in the new Big House. Abigail's niece, Louisa Smith, lived with them. In the summer, daughter Nabby arrived with her four children. Guests and friends arrived and departed, so the Big House sheltered between eleven and twenty people most nights, plus a Newfoundland puppy named Juno. It was a lively place. Abigail was at her best managing the meals and household, and the grandchildren were her special delight.

John rose at five or six every morning. He would clatter off with his ox and his low stone-hauling sled. With pry bars, drills, and chisels he laid New England field stone in logical, orderly, useful walls, straight as a string. And in the evening, he had Abigail and his books. What joy!

John still read newspapers, books, and magazines in English, French, Greek, and Latin. Abigail, too, was interested in current events. Their dinner table was a fascinating place for discussion on world events and grandchildren's adventures.

John and Abigail followed the unpredictable campaigns of Napoleon Bonaparte as he tyrannized Europe, reaching into Asia and Africa. John was glad that he had built up the United States Navy as a strong defense against Europe's troubles because the country was still young and frail. In 1804 they read that the political conspirator, Alexander Hamilton, had died as he lived: His scheming brought him into a duel with Jefferson's vice president Aaron Burr, who shot him dead.

The great pride in John's life was John Quincy's career as a public man. After an early career as a diplomat in the Netherlands, Johnny returned to practice law in Boston. He was quickly caught up in politics as a state senator, then as a United States senator for Massachusetts. He was a Federalist, as John had been, but his party was furious with him when he crossed party lines to vote for Republican

President Jefferson's giant scheme, the Louisiana Purchase. That enormous tract of land, bought from the French, opened the United States beyond the Mississippi as John Adams's negotiations with the British had opened the land between the Appalachians and the Mississippi River. John Quincy wrote to his father, "This would never had been possible, Father, if you had not made peace with France in 1800. I know what a sacrifice that peace was in your political career, but witness what a gift it was to our country."

In 1805, John replied to a letter from his old friend and Revolutionary colleague, Dr. Benjamin Rush. He began to write letters again with the old eagerness of his pen, great stacks of letters about things both important and trivial. He resumed work on the autobiography he had dropped for lack of interest. His years were mellowing him, and he was aware of what an annoying scold he must have been.

The year 1811 was bad for John and Abigail. Abby's sister, Mary Cranch, and their son Charles's widow, Sally, were dying of tuberculosis. John walked out one night to watch a comet, tripped on a stake, and gashed his leg to the bone; he was in bed for three months. Nabby had breast cancer and endured the ordeal of having the breast removed without anaesthetic. Richard Cranch, John's old friend who had introduced him to Abigail and had married her sister, died on October 10. Mary Cranch died the next day. John looked to the new year with as much hope as he could manage.

Perhaps that is why, on New Year's Day 1812, John wrote Thomas Jefferson for the first time in seventeen years. He wrote with warmth and affection, old disagreements faded, and Jefferson gratefully returned letters of his own. They began an enormous correspondence that discussed the old ideals of the American Revolution, the excesses of the French Revolution, their individual presidencies, world politics, Napoleon, and the future of the United States. They were two of the most learned, most experienced, most intelligent men in America examining their past and its effect on the nation they had helped to build.

Dr. Rush, who had encouraged both of them to

write one another for years, said to John, "I consider you and him the north and south poles of the American Revolution. Some talked, some wrote, and some fought to promote and establish it, but you and Jefferson *thought* for us all."

Dr. Benjamin Rush died in 1813 of typhus. Nabby came home to die of cancer, and Sally Adams, Charles's widow, died that year too. John was melancholy, and Abigail was nearly destroyed with grief.

John Quincy had been appointed as diplomatic representative to Russia, but he was called from St. Petersburg in April of 1814 to negotiate the peace treaty between Britain and the United States, concluding the War of 1812. The father negotiated the peace for one war, the son for another. Johnny was appointed as the United States diplomatic representative to Britain, a post his father had held before him.

In October 1818, Abigail Smith Adams was battling typhoid fever. John sat at her bedside for days before she died on October twenty-eighth, at the age of seventy-four. His partner, friend, advisor, comforter, and one of the most intelligent women of her age was gone. John said, "I wish I could lie down beside her and die too. . . . Her life has been filled up doing good." He was 83, but would not ride a carriage in her funeral. He insisted on walking behind the coffin in the procession to the meeting house cemetery.

John's remaining comforts were John Quincy's brilliant career, his grandchildren and great-grandchildren, and the letters from Jefferson. John felt trouble was brewing in "the way we enslave our black brothers. I fear that slavery might rend this mighty fabric of the United States in twain."

Then, in a letter, he wrote, "I am not weary of life. I still enjoy it. A great ice storm visited our farm, and, though it will ruin many of my fruit trees, I cannot help but love it. I have seen a queen of France with 18 million of *livres* of diamonds on her person, and I declare that all the charms of her face and figure, added to all the glitter of her jewels, did not make an impression on me equal to that presented by every shrub—the world was glittering with precious stones."

On February 9, 1825, John Adams's son, John Quincy Adams, became President of the United States. John was full of pride, yet had deep concern for Johnny. Visited by well-wishers in his library, he replied to their congratulations, "No man who ever held the office of President would congratulate a friend on obtaining it."

His life was peaceful and sweet. He was visited by his old girlfriend, Hannah Quincy Lincoln Storer, who had buried two husbands. They talked and joked with one another happily.

On July 4, 1826, the bells were ringing all over America, celebrating the fiftieth anniversary of the signing of the Declaration of Independence. John heard the bells, lying on his bed in his library, surrounded by his beloved books, and cared for by his granddaughter. "It is a great day. It is a *good* day," he murmured. He smiled. Before he breathed his last, John Adams said, "Jefferson survives."

But he did not. Jefferson had died a few hours earlier.

John Adams was a small, powerful, energetic man of exceptional inner sight and will. He was a

Swamp Yankee; the New England land and weather were in his bones, and the Puritan need to question, improve, and work drove him. His struggles for glorious things in the world were matched, in miniature, by his own struggles with vanity, doubt, and fear in his heart. He was often the most obnoxious, persistent, unpredictable man in Massachusetts—or Philadelphia, Paris, London, New York, or Washington. One of John Adams's great strengths was that he had Abigail Smith Adams as his partner. He was a loving father and husband, and a loyal friend. He thought of himself as a plain man of limited gifts born to "serious times" that demanded steely decision and stubborn determination. He had both.